Midnight Symphony

A.L. Kessler

© 2013 A.L. Kessler

Thank you to everyone that supported me through this journey, if not for you I wouldn't be here. Thank you to those who beta-read for me and helped turned this into a finished product. Special thanks to Jamie Wilson for creating my fantastic cover and encouraging me to keep going. Minion, you rock my socks off. Thank you for all the late night talks and crazy ideas, I don't think I would have the courage to do this without you. Brandon, my dear and loving husband, thank you for the massive amount of coffee and technical support.

CHAPTER ONE

The rain pelted Cora's hood as she made her way from her client's house. Reading the woman's cards turned out not to be as simple as she hoped. The client wanted more answers than Cora could provide and caused her to be late heading home. She carefully navigated her way over the cobblestone roads and checked down alleyways before passing them. Eyeing every shadow caused by flickering torches, she looked for the glinting of metal armor and flashes of the black cloaks of the guards, knowing it would do her no good to be caught by one.

She peeked around the last alley before the village square and her breath caught as she saw several guards corning some poor person. No, not person, witch. The magic crackled in the air, calling to Cora's own magic, reaching out for help, and raising the hairs on Cora's skin. Being caught by the guards risked her magic being bound - just the thought made her stomach churn. With a deep breath she ran past the opening of the alley, praying her shadow didn't catch the attention of the guards. She stood for a moment, listening for any sounds of alert; when only the sounds of the storm disturbed the night she continued on her way.

With the lack of people in the square this late at night, Cora easily ran across it, putting as much distance between her and the guards as she could. Almost to the docks on the other side, her foot caught on a raised cobblestone, and she let out a cry as she fell forward. Strong hands caught her around the arms, and she blinked at the armor clad chest in front of her.

A guard. Her heart dropped when she saw the insignia of the royal family. She froze in his grip, peeking from under her hood she waited for him to move. When his hands released her she straightened herself, batting at her skirts.

"Remove your hood, female." His deep voice rumbled through her.

Meeting his eyes, she debated her options. Water droplets clung to his dark hair, curling just under his ears, and soaked the blood red cape attached to his armor. He looked no more than thirty in human years. His face struck her as familiar, though he was rarely seen in the market place, the Prince. With a deep breath she pushed her hood back, revealing her mask.

His eyes followed the red and black design on it. "And your mask."

Panic flooded through her while she calculated her chances. She did the first thing she could think of; Cora wrapped her hand around his neck and pulled his lips to meet hers. She expected him to shove her away, instead he welcomed the kiss, cradling her head in his warm, strong hands, parting her lips with his tongue.

Heat rose in her and she pulled away, breathless, before it could go further. "Forgive me, sir, but I cannot." Glancing at his shocked eyes, she grinned before turning and running towards the docks. She pulled her hood back up as she stepped onto the gondola waiting there.

The boatman chuckled. "Your fare, Gypsy Lady?"

He held out a hand out to her, his long, skinny fingers curled up, forming a cup.

Pulling two silver coins from the pouch tied to her skirt, she glanced back where the prince had recovered from his shock and started towards the boat. She handed the coins to the ferryman. "Hurry, Leon."

He turned his blood shot eyes to the demon now running at them and chuckled shoving off the dock with his oar as the prince yelled for him to stop. The wooden paddle sliced silently through the water as Leon guided the boat down the stream, the current helping to carry them away from the town square and to the south village. Cora watched as the Demon Prince faded from view and then turned to the ferryman. "Thank you."

The man bowed his head and continued to push through the water. As the square faded, Cora thought about the Prince's reaction. He hadn't casted her away or cursed about her being a dirty magic user, or demanded for her to take off her mask again. No, the man decided to kiss her back and tried to push it further. Something deep in her clenched at the thought; she couldn't remember the last time a man showed her any true affection. Human or demon alike.

Most of the men in the village kept their distance because of the uncommon auburn hair and green eyes she inherited from her mother. When she ran around as the Gypsy Lady many men would flirt and dance with her, but none would be caught dead with a witch. To be caught with a witch with unbound magic meant possible death to a common villager. No one would risk it, not even for a night with the Gypsy Lady.

Not to say she'd never been with a lover. No, there were one here or there. Just none who sparked more than a tiny bit of passion in her soul. The Demon Prince however...

She licked her lips at the thought of the kiss, how his lips felt warm against hers, and it inspired heat to travel through her body making her muscles clench. At

—

the memory a new heat formed in her body and the cold night became too warm for her cloak.

Despite the mask, she dared not remove the hood of her cloak in front of the boatman's careful eye. As old and decrepit he seemed, his eyes showed a much more focused soul. He watched her as he navigated the straight river, taking her closer to her home.

Darius stood in the rain, staring at the dock where the boatman disobeyed him. Watching the woman in the cloak drift away left a funny feeling in him. One which he couldn't put his finger on. The blasted wench kissed him and he wanted more. He had pushed for it, but she rejected him with a flirtatious smile.

He recalled the way the moon played in her brilliant red hair and her vivid green eyes, framed by the mask. Black and red marks danced down the mask in an intricate pattern, making him wonder what it meant. As a woman, she broke the law to be out after the sun went down. Unless she carried the insignia of a whore, which he doubted with the way she held herself.

He finally started back towards the tavern where he left his horse. His father would be expecting him soon, and there would be hell to pay if he arrived late. He chuckled at the thought as he found his mount and untied the animal. Climbing on he debated about heading south where the woman did, but decided against it and turned his steed back to the north where the castle sat, looking over the human village. The towers with their arched windows and the surrounding wall stood out against the moonlight.

The bridge over the moat matched the same dark stone that climbed up the walls and towers of the castle. Beyond the outer walls lay the stables and barracks for the soldiers and guards, the smell of horses clung to the air.

As he approached the stables, various guards

whispered to each other, surprised to see the prince in this realm. Normally he stayed in the demon realm, but his father summoned him to the human realm, claiming he wanted to prepare Darius to rule.

A human woman came and gathered the reins of his horse, she glanced at him and then her gaze fell to the ground as he dismounted. He didn't bother with pleasantries, his mind still thinking about the warm lips he kissed earlier. His cock stiffened at the thought of kissing the masked woman again. He groaned and tried to shift himself without drawing attention to his groin.

When a male cleared his throat, Darius turned around to see who interrupted his fantasy. "Distracted?"

Darius met his father's eyes, seeing the same black pools he saw in the mirror; his father stood a few inches taller than he and had an angry scar across his left eye. "I had an interesting first night here."

"The village is normally quiet during the night. I heard my men caught a magic user, but no more than that." Xavier ran his hand over the stubble on his chin.

Darius chuckled. "A woman in a mask ran into me."

His father stiffened. "A red and black mask."

A statement, not a question. Darius raised a brow, curious. "How did you know?"

"That is the Gypsy Lady." Xavier's brows drew together. "It cannot be. She is dead." He laid a hand on the sword hilt at his side, as if comforting himself. Swiping a thumb across his lips, Darius shook his head. "She is very much alive, either that or a lively spirit. How do you know of this woman?"

"The woman you saw tonight, she is nothing more than a trouble maker, I will have to send my guards out for her."

A slight tick in the corner of his left eye, where the scar started alerted Darius to his father's lie. "You think her that much of a threat?"

—
7

"She just needs to be taken care of. You are dismissed." His father turned around without another word, the red tailored jacket bellowing around him like a cloak of blood as he entered the main part of the castle.

Darius tried to reason why the news of the masked woman would upset his father enough to storm off without further conversation, forgetting whatever he needed to tell Darius. He shook his head at his father's strange actions and then followed him.

Cora snuck into the small dwelling she and her sister called home. A one room cottage made of stone with a thatched roof where the door hung crooked, worn from the many years it hung there, but Cora didn't mind. This would always be her home. A curtain divided the room, creating an illusion of privacy for her sister when Cora came in from late nights and the girl's soft rhythmic breathing told Cora her sister was asleep.

Taking off her cloak, she hung it by the fireplace to dry. She reached behind her and untied the knot holding her mask in place. Holding it in her hand, she looked at it, her fingers brushed over the delicate design before she glanced in the mirror hanging over the mantelpiece. Though dust and dirt tinted the reflective surface, Cora could still see the matching marks scrolling around her left eye. The mark of not only a magic user, but a Demon Hunter. When the sun rose, the marks would fade, her hair would dull, and the green in her eyes would fade. With the coming of the day her tension eased, but it did not bring a stop to the hiding she detested. She placed the mask on her bed and returned to the fire with a sigh.

Next she took her corset off and then the shirt she wore under it, laying them both in front of the hearth to dry. She turned to the chest at the end of her bed, across from the fire and opened it before pulling out a nightdress. Dressing, she thought about the prince again and wondered why he came to this realm.

—

8

The festival of the full moon drew close, and she thought maybe he came for the celebration, but demons normally didn't attend. Only humans and witched participated in the festivities. She would grace the stage in the square as the Gypsy Lady and play her violin for the people, giving them hope of a day when the demons would no longer ruled. The people thought of her as a ghost of the past, from a time before the Demon King killed the human king.

She picked up the mask from her bed and went back to the chest. Pulling out a piece of black fabric, she wrapped the mask and placed it in the chest next to the wrapped violin. Part of her wanted the Prince to come to the festivities, but part of her knew once the Demon King learned the Gypsy Lady returned, he would be out to get her. With a sigh she crawled on her bed under the animal skin blankets and closed her eyes.

Seated at the table with the closest of his guards Darius held up his goblet of mead as one of them finished a toast to his arrival. He took a swig and set it back down on the table. Joy filled him as he sat with his guards; many of them came before him to the human realm to prepare for his arrival. Full of jest, he missed the company they provided.

"Heard a rumor tonight," one of them said, "while I was rounding up an unbound magic user."

Darius raised a brow. "Oh? Was the pesky magic user trying to exchange false information in an attempt to keep you from bind his magic?"

The soldier nodded. "Said the Gypsy Lady has returned, that she had been seen in the village."

"Impossible." Another one spoke up. "The Gypsy Lady hasn't been seen, except for at the full moon festivals. Though even then it can't be the same woman."

"Gypsy Lady?" Darius asked, leaning back in his chair.

—

The first one nodded. "A witchy woman, they say, a spirit to stir up hope in the human village. She plays the violin and bewitches anyone who approaches her." He chuckled. "She wears a mask to cover her face."

"Some say it is because it was scarred by a demon before she was killed and became a spirit."

"She is a magic user?" Darius asked. "Or a spirit?" Both of them shrugged. Darius' mind traveled to the woman he met in the square. He didn't recall the familiar hum of magic coming from her, though the heat of her lips his against occupied his memories for the night.

"You look as if you've seen a ghost, milord." The second one said.

Darius met his eyes. "Have you seen this Gypsy Woman?"

"I have, I've seen her dance on the stage in the moon light. I've seen her body move with the rhythm and capture the audience. We don't bother with trying to capture her during the celebrations. It would cause a riot among the people." The guard paused and Darius motioned for him to go on. "We are supposed to confirm if she is a magic user or not. If she is, the General has given us orders to bring her to the king. If not we let her be."

Darius sat back lost in thought. He never imagined the woman could be a magic user.

CHAPTER TWO

Theresa woke before Cora, and snuck passed the sleeping woman. Watching for a moment as her sister stirred under her sheets, fighting off some nightmare. A vision had come to Theresa the night before. Warning her of something to do with Cora and a demon, a strange foretelling of blood and magic she couldn't understand, yet.

Grabbing her cloak from the hook by the fireplace, she glanced once more at her sister, hoping Cora wouldn't wake before she returned. Theresa threw the cloak around her shoulders, pulling up the hood up as she headed out into the busy streets of the village.

As she made her way to the edge of the village, where the marketplace sat. Carts with produce and hand crafted merchandise lined the edges of the cobblestone roads and pathways, bustling with people shopping, many of them stopping to greet her. Some asked about her sister, who they knew about but never saw. Many of the people wore the bands around their wrists from the king, binding their magic, while others lived in fear and hid in the shadows.

"Good day," a male voice caught Theresa's attention and she swallowed as she met the handsome face of a demon. His stubble crossed over his chin from not being shaved that morning, the sun caught in his black eyes as he tried to meet hers, shaded by her hood.

She swallowed as she saw the royal seal on the chest of his armor and then bowed her head. "Good morning, milord. Is there something I can help you with?" She tried to squash the panic down, pushing away thoughts of being taken in as a seer or someone taking Cora away.

"Remove your hood." He grumbled, "What is with you people and your damn cloaks?"
She pulled her hood down, knowing the question didn't warrant an answer. The cold wind left by the storm whipped around her as she met his eyes in defiance.

Those dark eyes roamed her body, studying her and then he frowned. "Your name?"

"Theresa, sire." Her heart echoed in her chest as she wondered what he wanted.
He reached out, trying to cradle her face, but she stepped out of reach. He raised a brow. "You dare step away from the prince? Do you have no fear of the demons?"

"I am nothing but a simple human. I go about my business and you and your people normally leave me alone. Why should I fear you?" A simple lie she often told if she ran into a guard.

Darius stood in silence for a moment, still watching her. Theresa pulled her cloak tighter around herself to try to block the sting of the wind. When he said nothing more she pulled up her hood and started on her way. The Demon Prince didn't make a move to stop her and relief flooded over her. When she made it to the tree line at the edge of the market she glanced over her shoulder to make sure he hadn't followed before stepping into the woods.

She made her way through the evergreen pine trees and to a clearing. The early morning sun failed to penetrate the thick forest leaves making her shiver in the cooler, dense air. Leaning against a tree, she waited. Cracking sticks and crunching leaves made her stand straight and remove her hood, knowing the man she waited approached.

The hooded male walked into the clearing, with two others at his back. She caught a glimpse of swords when the cloaks parted, *Of course, his guard*, she thought.

"Greetings, Theresa."

She bowed her head to Lucas, the leader of the Demon Hunters. "I have come to talk to you about Cora."

All three of the figures in front of her tensed. Finally, Lucas spoke. "What of her?"

"Her marks have appeared and though her powers haven't increased I think you should take her into the clan and teach her."

"No."

The finality in his voice hit Theresa hard. "You don't understand, if her powers grow I will not longer be able to handle her or teach her. You will have to take on this-"

"She is not a Demon Hunter, she is not one of us." He snapped back.

Her fists clenched beneath the fabric of her cloak. "She has your blood, just because you abandoned her to me doesn't mean she isn't yours."

"Her powers are not strong enough. She will remain under your care."

Theresa couldn't help but notice he didn't deny the abandonment. "I have seen her in visions, the things that are to come, I cannot control it or her anymore." Lucas glanced back at the guards and then to Theresa. "Have you predicted that her powers will rise?"

"No, but she looks different in the visions. I do not

know why or what has caused it." She unclenched her hands. "You have to help her learn-"

"If you have not seen the rise in her powers, I have to do nothing. You are dismissed." He turned on his heels and he and the guards disappeared into the lush greens of the forest.

She cursed the man she called father, and the fact he refused to claim Cora as his own. Had Cora not been the product of infidelity than he would have no choice but to claim her and teach her as a Demon Hunter. Lucas resented the power not passing on to Theresa, making her a disappointment to him.

Pulling her hood up she started back towards the village, needing to get home before Cora woke.

Cora rolled over after tossing and turning; dawn came and went, but she didn't want to get out of bed. The long hours and misfortunes of the night before stayed with her, bringing another wave of exhaustion over her.

She heard Theresa leave before the sun rose to take care of business in the village. Cora groaned at the thought of explaining another lost client. Knowing she could replace the client with ease helped her push past the set back, but she knew her sister would worry about things. She could hear her sister's worried voice in her head: How would they buy food? Fabric for clothing? Replace the worn soles of the shoes Cora wore? Purchase strings for the violin?

Though older of the two, Theresa did nothing to earn money, not wanting to use her abilities for such reasons, but she watched out for Cora and the trouble the fates would bring. Theresa could be counted on to always be there to comfort and hide Cora when the king decided to raid the south village, looking for unbound witches.

Drawn out of bed by the dwindling fire, Cora coaxed the flames back to life with a log and poking it with the prod. The door to the cottage opened and she looked over to find her sister walking through the doorway, a bag from the market place clenched in her hands.

Cora stood and went to help her with it. "I hope this is enough to last us a while."

"You lost a client." Theresa meet Cora's gaze and gave an exasperated sigh.

The assumption her sister made hit something in Cora, making her want to argue, but she swallowed and took a deep breath instead. "Yes, but don't worry, there are others out there who want the services of the Gypsy Lady."

"There is also the Full Moon Festival tomorrow night, you will have coins tossed your way and tucked into your pouch all night. The people of the village love to see you dance and play on stage. They are most generous this time of the month." Her sister sighed as she set the bag down.

With the events of last night the festival must have slipped her mind. Cora smiled at her sister, glad for the reminder. "See we will be fine."

"That is the third one this season." Theresa stood with her back to the fire warming herself with flickering heat, her voice soft as she avoided her sister's gaze.

"The last two wanted to turn me in, this one wanted answers I didn't have. They think that magic is an all-knowing thing when it isn't. It is not my fault that they don't understand the craft." She sighed and pulled off her nightdress and donned her skirts, shirt and corset. "Did you have a good trip out to the market place?" Cora asked, not wanting to think about the lost clients.

Theresa stiffened and turned her front to the fireplace. "I ran into the Demon Prince while I was out."

Cora froze. What was he doing in the south part? Her lower body tightened as she thought about him.

"Cora?" Her sister asked, and then her eyes

—

15

widened. "You've already run into him."

A statement, not a question. Cora drew in a deep breath. "You promised to stay out of my head." She forced herself not to snap Theresa.

"You project too strongly for me to manage sometimes, but that's not the point. He saw you as the Gypsy Lady. You kissed him." Theresa shouted.

Cora licked her lips at the thought of the kiss and how she could have let it go further than a chaste kiss to distract him. She made her way over to the dusty mirror and ran her hand through her faded hair. The dark auburn, more red than brown, still contrasted against her sister's stark black hair. Cora liked the red hair of the Gypsy Lady more than her daytime counterpart. Her pale skin displayed no hint of the marks, but she traced her fingers over the spot as if willing them to appear.

"He is dangerous." Her sister continued. "Why did you let him get so close?"

Cora tried not to roll her eyes she backed away from the mirror and sat on her bed. "I didn't have a choice. It doesn't matter. He doesn't know who I am."

"And yet I have a feeling he is looking for you." Theresa crossed her arms. "Why else would he be here?"

"Maybe he plans on helping his father with the next raid." She sighed. "Don't worry. I won't be leaving the house until I have to meet another client down by the river tonight. It should be a quick trip."

Theresa raised a brow, trying to hide a smile. "And what does this client want?"

"The truth about his wife and her lovers." Cora started laughing. "She has six." And with that they dropped into an easy conversation about the town folks and their lives.

Darius paced through the square of the north village under the light of the moon, sticking closer to the docks. He spent his day wandering through the villages, trying to find anyone who looked like her, anyone with a

16

reason to hide their face, but he found none. The woman he met in the market place gave him a strange sense of familiarity, but he couldn't place from where. Part of him thought she might have been the woman in the mask, but her appearance didn't match up.
The woman in the mask held herself with confidence and if he could stand the two women side by side, he bet the Gypsy Lady would stand shorter. Maybe. Of course perhaps the spell she weaved helped with the appearance. He ran a hand through his hair and recalled the feline-green eyes shining from behind the mask, the other's held a hazel color.

Shaking his head he went closer to the river wanting to watch the current. A figure came into his view, a long cloak wrapped around her ankles as she walked allowing him a peek of the skirts she wore; he recognized his Gypsy Lady in a heartbeat. He ran down the banks towards her unsuspecting form, stopping only when she lowered her hood and looked up at the moon.

The way the moon glittered through the red strands made him think about the girl in the marketplace. Sneaking up behind her, he wrapped his arm around her waist from behind and used his other hand to tilt her head up to him. Before she could react he captured her lips, kissing her as he meant to the night before. His tongue teased the opening of her lips, begging to let him in. To his surprise she did.

Without thought or regret their tongues tangled until she pulled away with a gasp and met his eyes. The side of her face he could see flushed and it made him grow hard. He cupped a hand over the warm skin and smiled. "Hello, Gypsy Lady."

She stared at him speechless. When she seemed to have recovered she yanked her hood back over her head. "Forgive me, I lost myself for a moment."

"You turn away the affections of the prince?" He raised a brow and went to remove her hood again, anger filling him when she avoided it. He gathered her wrists in one hand and jerked her towards him. With his other hand he removed her hood and then reached behind her head, untying the knot holding her mask in place. He cradled the mask in one hand as he took in the sight of her. The same marks on her mask marched around her eye in red and black delicate lines and disappeared behind her ear into her hair. The reality of her being a magic user, and not an ordinary magic user, but a Demon Hunter hit him hard.

"Like what you see?" She snapped. He released his hands and cupped her cheek, brushing his thumb over the marks. His heart thudded in his chest. Training told him to kill her, but instinct screamed to kiss her.

As if reading his mind, she rose up on her toes and met his lips. He welcomed it, his hand move to cradle the back of her head and keep her pressed against him. A snarl escaped his lips when she pulled back.

"What do you want?" She asked, meeting his eyes.

"I want to know who you are."

She chuckled. "I am the Gypsy Lady, the voice of the spirits and the hope of humans and witches." With a wave of her hand, the mask left his grip and appeared in hers.

"Your name." He demanded, his fists clenching at his side.

"Come see me tomorrow before dusk, when the celebration begins and I will grant you an answer." She went to turn away from him, but he grabbed her arm as she did.

"Swear it?"

She seemed to think about it and then nodded. "You have my word."

He released her arm and let her disappear down the river, forcing himself to let her go before he kissed her again and possibly more. The thought hit him hard and groaned. "What is wrong with me?"

Cora stormed into the little dwelling, not bothering with being quiet. After the Demon Prince revealed her face she wondered how long it would be before he told the king. She placed the mask in the chest and sighed, though he saw her face and her marks he still returned the kiss. Not thrown off by it. She still felt his soft touch on her skin and would have done anything to let the kiss go further.

So she promised to let him know her secret, in the day light, when her magic would be at its weakest point. What had she been thinking?

A tingle danced down her spine when she spotted the bag holding her tarot cards, next to the violin. She snatched the bag up, the tingle turned to a hum of magic vibrating through her body and she knew it as a sign Fate wanted her to read. Opening the bag, she swallowed the fear when she saw the top card facing up.

The king of swords. The pale figure seemed to stare at her, his eyes changing from black to red and his hands gripped the sword in front of him. Her heart pounded in her chest as her breath hitched in her throat and in a rush she flipped the card over and shoved the deck back in the bag. When she closed her eyes, thinking on how to decipher the sign, the prince's face filled her vision. With his charming smile, he bowed and she could feel his lips on her hand.

The image shifted to him standing over the dead body of the Demon King, a sword protruding from the king's chest. Blood pooled on the floor of the stone room and inched towards her feet. A strange mix of confusion, relief, fear and pain tore through her body as she reached out for the prince, screaming "Darius."

With a gasp, Cora came back to herself, the pain and fear receding. Closing her eyes, she leaned her head against the wall wondering what message the vision held.

"You saw him again tonight." Theresa's voice broke Cora's silence.

"Yes. Have you heard from the others?" Cora spat the last word out.

Theresa shook her head. "Nothing of any substance. Don't worry about them though. You have your hands full. What did the Prince want this time?"

Cora shrugged. "Nothing. He kissed me again and I ran off."

"Do not lie." Theresa said. "There is no reason to hide things from me."

"There is no way to hide things from you." Cora corrected with a sigh. "He saw my face today."

Theresa froze and Cora met her eyes. "You can't disappear because of the festival tomorrow. The Prince will tell the king, the king will come for you."

Cora recalled the kiss the soft touches she shared with Darius and shook her head. "I thought that at first."

"And now?"

"Now I don't think he will. I don't think he wants to."

"You are putting a lot of faith into this."

Cora swallowed and looked down at the pouch with the cards. "I know."

CHAPTER THREE

Theresa held her head in her hands. Visions still invaded her mind. The blood trickled down her back, the echoes of a whip cracked through the room and the pain took her breath away. But it wasn't her back, her pain. The vision widened allowing her to see Cora against a wall, a demon at her back holding a whip dripping with red. Bile rose in Theresa's throat as Cora sagged in the chains. Her auburn hair stuck to her back. Coated with blood and sweat, she didn't flinch nor groan when another man approached her. The face of the man blurred by Fate, who granted Theresa the visions. She cried out when the vision switched again. Damp cool air touched her skin as stone walls appeared around her, the fire flickered but still chills cut through her.

The light bounced off the tarnished armor of a demon guard standing in front of the king. Red eyes blazed as the guard delivered news Theresa could not hear. The king rose and called out, soon another demon joined them. More orders came from the king and the two men left. The vision switched again and an ache in

Theresa's chest spread through her body as if it tried to tear her in half.

When the darkness cleared, a body wrapped in black mourning cloth came into view. Flowers tumbled from the stone slab displaying the body. Silver coins sat delicately on the wrapped face where the eyes would be. Weeping surrounded Theresa as the pain dragged her down and she reached towards the body.

"Cora." She shot up from her spot on the bed, sitting straight and trying to calm her labored breathing.

The emotions of the vision faded, allowing Theresa to clear her mind. With a few deep breaths, she banished the feeling of panic still bubbling below the surface. She needed to get Cora to agree not to go to the festival. Someway, somehow. She peeked around the curtain at the sleeping woman and sighed. Fate would not take away her sister. Theresa wouldn't let it.

Cora looked in the mirror as she placed her mask on her face. She could see Theresa standing behind her. Dark circles had formed under her eyes while a look of fear made them widen a bit.

"You know what is going to happen, correct?" Her sister's voice hesitated behind her. "Cora, the king will come."

"It wasn't the Prince who called him." Cora tied the knot and adjusted the mask. "I'm prepared for this. Whatever happens is what fate wants."

Theresa grabbed Cora's shoulder and spun her around. "The king will kill you." She hissed. "Is that what you want? Do you really think that Fate wants you dead?"

Cora sighed at the thought. "He won't kill me. He'll bind my magic." Her stomach churned at the thought and she grabbed her cloak trying to work through her uneasiness.

"Which is another way of killing you." Her sister snapped.

___

Cora spun and met her sister's eyes. "You were the one who said I couldn't disappear."

"But I did not know you agreed to meet with him before the festival."

Cora shrugged and tied the cloak around her shoulders. "It felt right."

Theresa came up and kissed Cora's cheek. "Go and play for the people. I'll keep the guards distracted if I can." She turned and picked up the violin off the bed before handing it to Cora. "Good luck."

Silently, Cora took the violin and the bow before walking out of the dwelling.

The boat bobbed outside the dock, Leon leaned against his oar, his eyes watching Cora as she came to him. She bowed her head to him. "Good evening."

"Good evening, Gypsy Lady. Are you ready for the celebration?" His voice cracked with age as he spoke to her and held out his hand to help her on the boat.

She smiled. "Of course."

"Your magic is at it's strongest tonight, when the moon rises."

His words soothed her and reminded her why she liked to appear on this night. The Demon King never ventured into the city during the full moon, the villagers believed he stayed away because he not could fight the combined power of the magic users. Though the sun still resided above the river, Cora could feel the magic buzzing through her.

She watched as people walked along the banks heading towards the north square. Some of them gawked and pointed. The Gypsy Lady out in the daylight. Cora pulled her hood up, covering her dull hair and eyes, knowing part of the fun for the people would be to see the transformation when the sun sank and the moon rose.

Leon dropped her off at the usual dock. She waited until he went to pick up his next passenger and

made her way further down the river, where she met
Darius the night before. The moon glinted off his armor
as he watched the people on the road above. With a
deep breath she approached him. "You look ready for
trouble."

"Should I not be? I hear that the magic users get
testy when demons are around for the festival. Even the
humans tend to be nervous." He met her eyes. "You
promised to tell me who you were tonight magic user,
and yet you come hiding your face."

"Witch, not magic user." She corrected him, before
looking around and removing her hood, then her mask.
She looked up at him, knowing her skin still remained
without the marks.
He studied her for a moment and seemed to stand taller.
"You are not the same woman from last night."

"I swear to you I am. I am the Gypsy Lady in the
true form. A spirit that changes at night." She held her
arms out. "You like my other form better?"

"I have a hard time believing you are a spirit.
What is your name?"
"Cora." The name dripped off her lips. "I have kept my
word, now I must go. The village is expecting me."

He reached out and cupped her cheek, his hand
felt rough against her skin, but the familiar feeling made
her body clench. He leaned in to kiss her, but stopped
just shy of her lips. "I will see you after. You have my
word." He stepped away and marched up the hill to the
street.

Cora's breath escaped her as she tried to process
what happened. The desire to rush to him and run her
hands through his hair and devour his lips with a kiss
went through her. The clenching inside her stomach
told her she'd be willing to go much further, because he
didn't turn her away. A demon who wanted to be with a
witch, it sounded like a joke. She replaced her mask
and hood and went up to the streets, weaving her way
through the crowd.

As she approached the square the energy in her bubbled. The bustle of the people around her, the exciting gasps as she passed by them and the hum of other witches in the area helped feed the thrill of being among them as the Gypsy Lady. She ran towards the stage and leapt on to it with her violin. Drawing the bow across the strings, a smile crossed her face while the note echoed though the square. With a toss of her head, her hood fell back around her shoulders and she started to dance across the stage while she played.

Darius watched from the back of the crowd as Cora feet carried her across the stage in a fury of skirts and her cloak. Her hair swirled around her as she danced and played, catching the fading sunlight.

"You are taken with her." The soft feminine voice made him look next to him. Theresa, the woman he met in the market place stood there, arms crossed and eyes glued to the stage.

He snorted. "She is beautiful and entrancing, if that is what you mean."

"No. I know that you have kissed her and how you crave to run your hands over her naked body." She made a face and shook her head.

The thought shot straight through him. "You speak as if you know her personally."

"I don't, I can just...see it in the way you watch her." She glanced at him and fidgeted with her hands.

He raised a brow. "Are you lying to me?"

"No. Why are you even here? I didn't think that the demons came to this festival." She looked back to the stage to watch Cora dance.

The new melody started out slow, melancholy, but started to pick up speed as she made her way across the stage. Darius shrugged. "I wanted to see the Gypsy Lady dance. I hear this monthly celebration is the only time that humans and magic users seem happy."

"Witches, the term magic users will offend people."

—

25

That struck a cord, a bit of anger rose up in him. "Did I offend you peasant?"

"No, milord." She bowed her head, reacting to the reminder of her place in life.

He took a few steps towards the stage, wanting to get closer, but a light grip on his wrist made him stop. He looked back at Theresa, noticing her glazed over eyes, a look he often saw in the oracles' eyes. A seer. Not daring to pull away, for fear of interrupting her vision he could not break contact. Her fingers left his wrist and she started to move towards the stage. "Cora!"

Darius pulled the woman back to him by her arm as guards flooded the stage. Cora ran for the edge of the stage to jump into the scattering and screaming crowd. A demon in full demonic form landed on the stage behind Cora. Towering over her while his talon like feet dug into the wood of the stage, causing it to crack and creak under the weight of the massive beast. A snarl came out of his muzzle-like mouth as he reached for the girl. Cora cried out as the demon snatched at her arm with its claws. The violin clattered to the ground when he threw her to a guard.

The crowd continued to scatter, going around Darius and Theresa. He turned her. "Go."

"I can't leave her. He'll kill her." She shrieked and tried to yank her arm out of his grasp.

He tugged on her arm. "I won't let him. Now get out of here before he realizes what you are too." He shoved her into the fleeing crowd and made sure she went to the river. He turned back to the scene on stage where the demon started to revert back into his human-like form.

Another demon in full armor, Xavier, stood behind Cora now. "You want to see who your Gypsy Lady truly is?" He snarled at the crowd.

No one stopped, no one watched, except for Darius and another man to his left. Darius spared the man a glance, taking in the clenched fist and the tight jaw of the strange man, before turning back to the stage. The guard holding Cora forced her to her knees before Xavier ripped off her mask. Almost as if out of instinct she bowed her head to let her hair cascade over her face.

The guard summoned something to his hand and clasped it around Cora's wrists. She cried out in pain and Darius knew the binds on her wrist bound her magic. He could see her struggling to control her breathing and her temper on stage.

"Take her to the dungeon for the night, I'll deal with her tomorrow." The guards dragged her of stage. Cora struggled against them trying to get loose, but they held strong.

CHAPTER FOUR

Darius stormed into the foyer of the castle. Seeing his father sitting in front of a fire, he roared, "What were you thinking? Raiding the festival?"

"It needed to be done, it was the only way I was going to catch that whore." Xavier leaned back in his chair. "But I do not think that is the same Gypsy Lady that the guards have been speaking of."

Darius raised a brow and went to take a seat next to his father. "Oh? It would be a shame to go through all that trouble and have the wrong girl."

"No, one more dirty magic user off the street. These people are trouble Darius, do not let the weak ones fool you." He folded his hands and placed his chin on them as he gazed into the fire. "This woman should have been able to resist my own magic if she was the true Gypsy. Simply because she should carry the Demon Hunter's blood in her."

Darius shrugged. "You bound her magic, that may have weakened the actual powers of demon hunting. Not to mention they say that she changes at night, much like spirits." He thought back on the words of his guards and Theresa. Through his study of histories he could recall no mention of the Gypsy Lady.

"You believe their silly little stories?" Xavier laughed. "You are more naive than I thought."

Darius shook his head. "I'm not naive, you may learn something if you listen to the people. They say that the gypsy's hair and eyes change as her powers grow at night. That would account for the differences between the girl today and the girl I saw last night, same with your guards. There was an old legend that said that the Demon Hunters were stronger at night, because it helped them hunt us during our heightened time."

"So what are you saying?" Xavier looked at his son. "I will not take the binds off her to see if her magic comes out at night."

He thought for a moment. "You may not have to. Let me monitor her for the day and night and I will let you know if there are any changes."

"I will let you have her as a servant, but I am sending you back to the demon realm with her."

He frowned. "That is sure to get her killed."

"The oracles there will be able to help you in you mission of finding out what the girl is. The guards will leave her alone as long as she is with you." Xavier said easily and then motioned to the door. "Shall we?"

Again, a nagging feeling developed in the back of Darius' mind telling him his father was hiding something. He moved to the door, trying to think of how to use this to his advantage.

The cold stone bit into Cora's skin while she knelt in the middle of the cell waiting. Bars kept her trapped in the small square and she wore herself out pacing the night before. Her features remained plain through the night and her magic remained quiet as the pain from the binds still hummed through her veins.

Cora looked up, feeling her anger swell when

Xavier and Darius walked in, flanked by guards. "What did you do to me?"

"You do not like being under my power?" Xavier laughed. "You are not as strong as everyone thinks you are, Gypsy."

Cora batted her eyes at them. "Take these bands off and maybe I am." She held her wrists up to him. "Let me free, or do you really fear me Demon King?"

"I fear no magic users." He said, "Normally I kill them. This time my son has begged me to spare your life until we find out if you are truly the Gypsy Lady of the night that everyone speaks of."

Her eyes flickered to the prince and then back. "Meaning?"

"You are going with him to the demon realm until we get our answer." The king said, wrapping a hand around a bar. "Even if you manage magic, you will have no chance to escape." When he removed his hand the bars disappeared. He snatched Cora's wrist and threw her towards Darius who caught her without effort.

Cora tried not to panic; even if she managed magic the other demons would kill her in an excruciating manner. With a deep breath she pulled away from Darius, steadied herself and tried to smooth out her skirts. "This should be a challenge then, won't it?"

"Don't push him." Darius' sharp voice cut through her false confidence. "He could be cutting you down right now. He's being nice enough to give you the benefit of the doubt."

Cora took a shaky breath. "Don't want to kill too many plain magic users, it looks bad to the humans." She concluded.

Xavier snarled. "Take her before I change my mind."

Darius grabbed her wrist and in a shift of magic, the dungeon disappeared only to replaced by stonewalls covered in tapestries. Stepping up to one, Cora studied a magic user with similar marks stitched on the face. Hands rose in the air, fire seemed to follow the character's motions. Before her a line of demons, some lying on the ground, arrows through the chest and others advancing. Behind the woman, a line of other witches were wove, some with simple colors to depict what they controlled. "Those are Demon Hunters that they are fighting."

"Of course they are. Back then, regular magic users knew better than to get on the field, but Demon Hunters were higher in numbers. Now they are rare to find." He looked at Cora. "And most of them are very well hidden."

Cora shrugged. "Because the demons managed to kill most of them off. The rest of the bloodlines were smart and went into hiding to bide their time."

"Do you know where they are hiding?" He asked.

The question didn't surprise her and she shook her head. "They don't care about me because I don't show any real signs of being a hunter, just like my sister." Pain struck her in the chest as she thought about Theresa. She wanted to be home consoling her sister. Who would be there to bring in the money for the food, who would cover for her sister when the visions came unexpectedly?

"You won't betray my sister. Promise me. I saw you two talking at the festivals. She's not truly a magic user, she's only a seer."

"You know that we have uses for seers here right?" He smirked and started down the hall. "I suggest that if you want to live you follow me."

When he arrived at the end of the hall, he threw open the large oak doors. Cora walked in and looked around. Lavish red fabric flowed over the window in the gentle breeze and complimented the black silk sheets draped on the four-poster bed.

"Not much of a cell." She said lightly, ignoring his earlier comment about seers knowing it would only bait him.

Darius shook his head. "This is my chamber. If I left you in the cells here you wouldn't last the night, especially if you change. So you'll sleep here, in my room."

"Like a pet?" She asked, running her hands over the soft wood of the bed. The thought of being in his room with him so close caused moisture to appear between her legs.

He shrugged. "Think of it as you will, but either way this is safer." He opened the curtains revealing a blood red sunset. "So when do your powers normally show, Gypsy?"

"I have a name." She followed him and looked out the window. Ruins littered the land in front of her and the sunset cast a strange glow on the streets. Demons moved through the maze-like city as she tried to recall myths and stories of the demon realm. She crossed her arms at an unfamiliar feeling crawling through her.

Darius smiled over the land, "Cora, and it is a beautiful name, but it ruins the mystery of the Gypsy woman."

His hand touched her hair and a familiar tingle ran through her body. She dropped her arms to her side, welcoming the hum of magic starting in her chest and exploding through her body.

He turned back towards her and he smiled. "Just like a true Demon Hunter. Look at you, my father was only fooling himself to think that the bands would be able to contain your magic." He spun Cora to face the full-length mirror. A smile crossed her face as vibrant red cascaded through the auburn hair, taking it over and pure green spread over the dull hazel of her eyes. The tattoos crawled across her face, bringing with it a rush of magic pushing through her and against the bonds on her wrist. She met Darius' eyes in the mirror as they flashed red and followed the lines of body. His handsome jaw framed by black hair begged to be kissed.

When she turned around to fulfill her urge, he stepped out of her reach and looked away from her.

"You are beautiful for a human."

"And you are handsome for a demon." She whispered, but in a louder voice added, "I am no mere human, I'm a witch."

"A Demon Hunter, even. How have you managed to keep yourself hidden so long?"

She shrugged and looked down at the iron bonds on her wrist. Running her hand over the smooth metal she tried to find a weakness she could use to remove them. "My family doesn't believe that I hold the right blood and left me with my sister. Since then Theresa and I have been in charge of each other's safety. Neither of us have had contact with the family since they left us."

"So you knew that you might be a Demon Hunter." He turned his back towards her, "and yet you still go gallivanting around the squares as if you are nothing but a normal magic user."

"Witch." She corrected again with an irritated snap. "And I do not gallivant. I go out and find work, doing parlor tricks like reading cards and palms, that sort of thing. I have to earn money so Theresa and I can eat. Theresa, though stronger than me doesn't have as much control over her power."

"She's not stronger than you. She doesn't have the same genes as you. You got the demon hunting ones."

"I don't even know what that really means. I have only heard the terms, and it's been hinted at that I might be one."

"You need to spend more time in the library or something." Darius shook his head. "A Demon Hunter is a powerful magic user that used to fight-"

"I know what one is. I don't know what it means to be one, or how the powers are passed down." She snapped and then started pulling on the bands.

He turned to her, "they won't be coming off

anytime soon. They need to stay there to help the illusion that you aren't a Demon Hunter and are just...special."

"You aren't going to run off to daddy and tell him what I am so he can kill me?" She batted her eyes at him masking the fear balling in the pit of her stomach.

"I don't think you are worth killing, not yet at least."

Theresa rushed through the trees, slapping at the branches and brush blocking her path. She demanded out loud for her father to appear as she tripped on a root. Panic and fear coursing through her body forced her to continue forward until she broke past the border of the clearing. She couldn't handle the events of the night before, she needed help and guidance on what to do about Cora being with the king. If the group would not be willing to help her, at least they would be warned.

"Looking for me, daughter?" The familiar male voice caused her to freeze, the unfamiliar term catching her off guard.

"I am. Something has happened."

"They say that the Gypsy Lady has been captured, is that what you are referring to?" No emotion sounded through his voice.

Theresa could have smacked him for his lack of caring. "They took her from the stage during the festival. I don't know if they killed her. At the very least they bound her magic." A whole new fear threaded through her muscles, causing her to tense. "I can't sense her, I can't see her."

"Relax little one, you told us that she was more powerful than we all had thought. That you had seen a future with her in it." He stepped forward. "Did you not?"

Theresa nodded. "I did, but things have shifted, I don't know if she will live, I can't see anything past her and the prince."

"The prince?"

She hesitated for a heart beat. "The Demon Prince."

"You saw her with him how?"

"I don't know if I should share that with you. The details are not clear."

The man chuckled. "Scared for your sister? You fear us Theresa, but we are only trying to protect you and her from the fate that we have been dealt."

"You could change that fate if only you would train others to fight the demons as well."

"Do not speak of what you do not understand. Now tell me how you saw Cora with the prince. I do not like the context that your voice offered."

Theresa weighed her options, knowing other seers worked among the ranks of the Demon Hunter, but guilt of hiding knowledge began to overtake the fear in her chest. She took a deep breath. "I saw them laying naked together in a pool of black, there was a circle around them-"

"Sex magic." He hissed.

"But there was also blood involved, so I don't know exactly what kind of magic it is. Cora is trained in neither, nor has she shown interest in them." She rushed the words, not wanting her father act rashly. "I do not know what it means, but before she was taken, I could see her standing in front of the people, in full glory. No cloak around her, no mask to cover her marks, and they were cheering, but now...now it all seems to have faded. Like I can no longer see her future."

He reached a hand out to her and stroked her cheek, his skin cold against her flushed cheek. "You have grown strong in your visions, my dear little one, but you have not grown strong enough to see past what Cora may or may not choose. There are new elements now that were not meant to come into play. Those are interrupting the visions."

"But what of Cora, is she still alive?" The heavy feeling of grief made its way through her body. "I do not like the idea of my sister sitting in a damp dungeon, powerless, and waiting to be killed."

"She is still alive, and at this time she is well, but Fate has some plans for her, and now that she is in their realm there is nothing that we can do to help her."

"Their realm? You mean that she is no longer in our world?" Theresa put a shaking hand to her mouth trying to keep her panic in.

He nodded and then looked behind him. "You must go, the Demon King will be visiting your home. Get rid of any evidence of Cora that you can, even her violin."

"But-"

"I know, but that will give you away instantly and we cannot afford to have you both under the king's powers. Now go." He faded into the darkness of the trees behind him.

Theresa gathered herself and ran back into the village and to their home, swiftly throwing anything Cora wore or touched into the fire. She picked up the violin and hesitated as she held it towards the flames. Pulling it back to her chest she tried to stop the tears forming in her eyes. Her sister would never forgive her for burning the only link to her mother. Theresa sighed and spied the chest where she kept the extra blankets and cloaks. Frantically she buried the violin within the fabric. With a chant and a wave of her hand, she concealed the whole thing from view.

Theresa sat on her doorstep watching pinks and reds paint the sky as the sun rose for the day. Her mind drifted to Cora, wondering if her sister could see the same hues or how it differed in the demon realm. The uncommon and unpleasant clattering of horses' hooves pulled her from her thoughts. The soft thud of wheels made Theresa look up; the black carriage stopped in front of her dwelling. Theresa rose to greet the guest she knew resided inside. She bowed low as the king stepped out of the carriage.

"Cleaver woman knew we were coming." He whispered. "I hear you know the Gypsy Lady well."

Theresa shrugged. "I have been to many of her performances."

"Search her house and let me know what you find." He snapped at the guards before he grabbed Theresa's wrist and yanked her away from the door. "I saw you chatting with the prince at the festival."

"He believed I could provide him the answers that he sought about her change."

"So you believe those silly tales about her?" He asked as the guards filled the small dwelling and started tearing through things.

Theresa tried not to cringe at the harsh sounds of crashing glass and splintering wood. "They are not silly tales. The Gypsy Lady is very much a part of history. I'm sure you can even recall watching her dance in the squares during the night before you completely took over."

The king dropped her wrist as if it burned. "It cannot be the same woman."

"Why not?" She asked, casting her eyes towards him. "They claim that she is a spirit."

A snarl escaped through his pressed lips. "Because I killed that whore the night that I found she had borne a child to a Demon Hunter."

Theresa nodded. "I ask again, why can it not be her? If she is a spirit perhaps she comes around to haunt you and remind you of the guilt you feel."

He backhanded her. "Do not talk to me as such, you filth."

Theresa stumbled from the blow the sting of it making her eyes tear up. She kept her head bowed as she tried to recover. The guards came back out of the home. "She is clean, nothing here to link her to the gypsy."

"Take her anyways. She knows something." He snapped turning from her as a guard grabbed her wrists. Theresa dug her heels into the ground and tried to yank her arms away from the man pulling her towards the carriage. In the end he overpowered her and shoved her in before the horses headed towards the castle.

CHAPTER FIVE

Cora looked over the book Darius brought her from the library the night before. She used the book and its tales to distract her from the itching need to perform magic. She twirled a piece of auburn hair around her finger while she flipped the page. The images of demons and witches printed on the page did nothing to calm the uneasy feeling in her gut.

The door to the chamber clamored open and Darius walked in with several guards. Cora looked up and shut the book.

With a smirk, Darius held his hand out to her. "Come along."

Gathering her skirts with one hand as she slid off the chair, she sauntered towards him, but refused his hand. "Are we going on a walk?"

"Something like that. My father would like to see you." He grabbed her wrist, his jaw tightening as he yanked her out of the room.

She tried to pull out of his bruising grip, the churning in her gut flipped to a sickening panic. "Does this mean we are going back to the human world?"

———

"No, he took a trip here. Do not fight me on this, Cora." His fingers tightened and a bolt of pain ran through her arm.

The pain reminded her of her captivity and it would be best to mind her manners. She nodded and followed him, letting her arm go limp.

The guards led them through winding halls of stone, some covered in tapestries and others bare. Torches bounced shadows off the walls as they passed, acting as the only light for their path. Cora's eyes traveled over all the different doors and passages they passed. "This place is a maze."

"It is, another reason that you cannot walk around on your own here. You will get lost." He moved one of the tapestries and revealed a staircase.

She hesitated as an armed guard started up the stairs but she followed him with Darius right behind. He kept a gentle hand at the small of her back to keep her balanced as she climbed the steep stairs. "Where are we going?"

"To my father's foyer. He says he discovered something interesting and he wants to test it against your knowledge." He watched as the door at the top opened and the guard disappeared inside.

Cora took a deep breath and walked in. Strong hands grabbed her shoulders and forced her to the ground. Her knees hit the ground with a thump and a rough palm forced her head into a bow. She tried to recover her senses as black boots came into her view.

"Tell me the story of the Gypsy." The king's voice demanded.

Cora closed her eyes. "I don't know all of it. It started centuries ago, there was a woman that would dance by the riverside with her violin, entrancing the travelers with her music. No one knew who this woman was or where she had come from. She simply appeared. She continued to appear with each generation."

"And you are the current generation." He said

simply. "You're Aura's daughter."

Every muscle clenched at the name she hadn't heard in years. She couldn't stop the widening of her eyes or the catch in her breathing. "I don't know who you are talking about."

"Come now, I can see how you took that news. Your body tensed, your breathing hitched," he moved behind her and the guard let up so she could move again. "So tell me, how old were you when I killed that whore?"

Gritting her teeth against the swell of anger in her, she bit out an answer. "I don't know who or what you are talking about." Pain exploded in her scalp when her hair was pulled and her head yanked back. She met the black eyes of the king, snarling at him.

"You have her eyes, her hair, her body even. How old were you?"

Cora swallowed as the grief made her heart ache with the memory of her father walking into the dwelling that night and telling her without remorse how the Gypsy Lady's body had been discovered on the bank. She took a shaky breath. "I was five when she was found dead."

"And your father? Where is he?" Xavier let her hair go, and she rolled her neck.

"I don't know. He left me with my sister when I showed no signs of carrying the gene he was looking for. I was his biggest disappointment." She tried to keep it lighthearted, but bitterness crept into her tone.

Xavier laughed. "Ah yes, your sister Theresa, the seer. She's just as strong willed as you are."

The anger shot through her and forcing her actions. Cora leapt up, snatching the sword from the guard and went to strike Xavier. With a calm wave of his hand, Xavier froze her in mid motion, her breath shaky and her eyes burning. Pain weaved itself through her body, causing her muscles to contract as she tried to fight against his magic.

"You care greatly for your sister; do not worry I have not harmed her. She has been a charm to work with." He said with a laugh. "I was even nice enough to get the oracles to help her with her powers. You on the other hand, have yet to show us the true potential that lies within you, and it's only a matter of time before I have to decide what to do with you." He paced the room and stroked his chin.

"So you will encourage my sister to grow, but kill me if my powers show?"

"She is a seer, you are a magic user. You may have the potential to be a Demon Hunter, something I do not want alive."

She chuckled and tried to ignore the pain in her chest it caused. "We share the same blood. If she is not a Demon Hunter neither am I. So you should just unbind me and let me go."

"You're not that lucky." He paused in front of her and stroked her cheek. "You look so much like your mother that I have a hard time believing that you do not have the marks of a Demon Hunter."

Cora turned her face away. "Maybe it wasn't from her side."

"Now, now, Cora, Demon Hunters do not breed with normal magic users." He clicked his tongue at her. "Now my son shall keep an eye on you. Once you show any signs I will know. I have eyes and ears all over this castle that are loyal only to me." He looked at Darius. "Now keep in mind that if you fail me in this, it is your skin that I will have." He turned his back to them.

Cora dropped the blade when she could move again, but took a step forward. Darius' hand on her arm caused her to hesitate. "Come on, it's time to leave." He spun her around so she faced the door and led her back down the stairs.

Theresa came away from her vision with a gasp. Her body ached from the amount of magic and seeing the king demanded of her upon her arrival. Despite the sitting pillow she knelt on, stiffness grew in her knees as she perched on the edge of a large pool of water. Deep depths free of reflections and ripples, the long lane of water stretched half the length of the room with kneeling pillows dotting the edges for other seers.

"Now look in the water, young one, and tell me what you see." The old crone's voice was a soft whisper in the chamber, as if she didn't want to disrupt the air around them.

Theresa leaned over and peered into the water. Cora's face appeared with the black and red marks of the Demon Hunter mixing with crimson blood. "My sister and she's hurt."

"Widen your sight, see more than just her."

She took a deep breath and forced her mind to pull back, widening the vision to give her more than her sister. Xavier stood behind Cora, a wicked smirk on his face as his blade caught the gleam of the fire when he raised it. "No!" Theresa reached out and fell into the pool shattering the image with her body. She came to the surface sputtering and then clung to the edge of the pool. The water chilled her to the bone but did nothing to chase away the shock from the vision.

"You must learn that visions are not real-time. That is if you wish and have the ability you can change the future." The oracle held a hand out to help her out of the pool. "You must calm yourself. Your sister is your biggest weakness."

Theresa took the offered help out of the water and twisted her hair so water cascaded from it and onto the tiled floor. "I'm used to getting visions moments before the event happens, but I guess there is really no use in these visions right now anyways."

"Now you know that is not true." The woman summoned a towel and draped it over Theresa's shivering shoulders.

"This tells me otherwise. I know that it is rare

—

43

that you can change the future, so don't try to give me false hopes." She patted and rubbed the droplets of water off her skin with the towel. "Cora is with the demon royal family, and that means that her life is constantly in danger."

"You need to let go of thoughts of your sister, it will clear your mind and your senses and you can focus on seeing other things." The woman cooed.

Theresa glared at her. "Like the things the king wants me to see, how the wars will end, where the hunters are."

"That will spare your life."

"And that is what is important here," she whispered going back to her kneeling pillow. She closed her eyes and tried to clear her mind. If she lived maybe a chance to save Cora would show itself.

Lucas walked through the halls of the cave he had called home for twenty years. The lack of contact from Theresa worried him and a soldier brought word back that the king had a Demon Hunter and it wasn't one of Lucas'. Instead it was a female, one of the few left, and he refused to believe that the king lacked knowledge and thought Cora to be a Demon Hunter. Other rumors spoke of a new seer the king took in. Lucas needed to send a scout to Theresa's house, but it would be too risky if the guards beat him there.

"It is time Lucas," A female voice came from behind him. "She won't be able to fight the pull anymore."

"She isn't a Demon Hunter, Elsie." He stated and his steps never faltered as if he wished to leave the female behind him. "The one I am worried about is our daughter."

She followed him. "Theresa is cunning and will be able to take care of herself if she's in a situation."

"Cora is normally the one who bails her out of

things." He shook his head. "If Theresa is with the king, then he knows that she is a seer, and it is only a matter of time until she leads him to us."

"She would never betray us."

"Not on purpose she wouldn't, but the king can be very manipulative. I will send out scouts to her house to make sure she is alright at dusk, so they can conceal themselves."

"And if the guards are there?"

Lucas shrugged. "Then we are going to have to find another way to rescue our child."

"Children, you will not abandon Cora there."

He raised a brow. "She isn't even your child, and you care to rescue her?"

"She is your child, you should want to rescue her." She shook her head. "Do what you must, but do not abandon either child there. Not like you did after Aura died."

Lucas nodded and entered the main cavern. Shelves stacked with overflowing books lined the cave. He went to the furthest shelf and ran his fingers over the fading titles of the leather bindings, searching for a particular one among the dust. "It has been centuries since there has been a break in the Gypsy Lady lore."

"What does that fairy tale have to do with anything? It was merely meant to keep Cora busy and give her a way to hide herself."

He paused at a thick black book. It took little work to free the book from the shelf. He held it in one hand and flipped through pages with the other. "Aura was one of the gypsy ladies, she passed it down to Cora when she was killed. The violin was a piece of her past, part of her family."

"That still doesn't explain to me what it has to do with any of this." She crossed her arms. "You are speaking in riddles."

Lucas held the book up. On the page in black and white stood a gypsy wrapped in the wings of the demon standing behind her. "The original Gypsy witch came from the demons." He studied her brown eyes, waiting for a reaction.

"Still not understanding." Brushing her long dark hair over her shoulder, she took the book from him and studied the picture.

He sighed. "She came from the demons, a child of a demon and human. She was cast from both worlds, and from there she became the mother of the Demon Hunters."

"If Cora is a direct descendant of the original Gypsy Lady then she should be a Demon Hunter. But she doesn't show any potential."

He shook his head. "That's the lie we told her and Theresa and then began to believe ourselves. The fact that her magic marks her during the night means that she has the potential. Something just needs to wake that power up."

"Which would be what?" Elsie asked studying the ancient script under the image.

He sighed. "We don't know, there hasn't been a true Demon Hunter descendant like her in many years. It is different for each hunter."

"And when your powers woke?" She asked.

He shook his head. "Mine was a near death situation."

"You didn't talk to her about that?"

He glared at her. "Not exactly dinner conversation." He snapped. "Do you want to talk about when your powers were awaken?"

She blushed and turned away.

"That's what I thought."

Cora snuggled into the fur while in her dreams she saw Darius tucking it around her and kissing her head before disappearing out the door. When the audible sound of a lock clicking Cora woke with a jump. The wind from the open window whipped through the

---

lonely room as she sat up wondering where Darius ran off to. She knew no guards stood outside the door and after seeing the castle she understood why, but with Darius gone, her chance to scheme and plan an escape came.

A pulse started through her and turned to a hum as her magic played in her while the moon rose higher into the cold night. Going to the window to shut the open glass a need started to curl inside her stomach combined with a thrill to perform some sort of magic. She knew what she wanted to do, create a trap for Darius. One not meant to hurt the demon, only keep him from hindering her escape. Turning to the dead coals in the fireplace she grinned and went to it.

Cora carefully dug through the ashes to retrieve a coal. Drawing a careful line she tested it to make sure it marked and wouldn't crumble in her hand. Satisfied with the trail of ash it left she went to work. With practiced and careful strokes she created a circle around the bed. Each line and rune she drew held a purpose in the design and stood out against the gray stones. Her confidence made her feel Darius would simply overlook the circle, thinking her too weak to trap him.

She threw the coal back in the fire and used the washing room to clean her hands. With nothing to do but wait she lounged herself on the bed and settled in with the book on demon history. The lock on the door clicked and the hinges creaked as it opened, but she didn't bother looking up at the demon she knew stood there.

"Been a busy little magic user tonight, have we? " He shook his head and stepped right into the circle.

Cora waited for the familiar tingle to come. When nothing happened she looked up at Darius with wide eyes.

"You look surprised, you thought your magic was strong enough to hold me?" He laughed. "You silly, silly girl."

She closed the book, mentally cursing her failure. "Can't blame a girl for trying."

"No, but had it been my father who walked in instead of me he would have killed you instantly." He started to rub the circle out with his foot.

She raised a brow, "and you aren't going to kill me?"

"You've just shown yourself as weak." He sat down on the bed and looked over her shoulder. "I'm glad to see you're studying."

Any confidence she gathered faded at his statement. "It's all very fascinating, and it's not stuff that we're taught in the human world, even as witches. It seems that our histories complement each other, strange how we're never taught the other side of things." Despite the blow to her ego, she wanted to lean back into him in hopes he would comfort her. Her body craved another one of his luscious kisses or even a brush of his fingertips here or there.

He shrugged. "Apparently none of our people are. Your sister is doing well."

"You saw her?" She jerked her head to look at him and meet his eyes, searching his face for a hint of a lie.

"She's working with an oracle to increase her powers. She's doing very well." He moved away from her and to the window.

"That means that she's here. How could she be in this realm and you not mention it to me before?" She slid off the bed and followed him.

"Because you're not supposed to know. My father wanted me to tell you that she was dead, he thinks it would bring out your powers."

Cora shook her head. "From what I understand, if I don't have those powers now then I won't have them, ever."

"Not true."

"Says the demon who has rarely been in the

human world." She countered and ran a hand through her hair. "She is well though?"

He nodded. "She is not harmed in anyway."

"Good, very good, she's not very talented when it comes to getting herself out of trouble. At least she seems to be managing to survive."

"I just came to make sure that you were surviving the night, speaking of, and not thrashing about on the floor during a spell. I must get going, I have a meeting with my father in the human world tonight." He went to the wardrobe and pulled off his shirt. A scar crossed his back standing out against his skin.

Cora stood and went to touch it. "What is that from?"

In a flash he spun around and grabbed her wrist. "Do not touch it." He snapped. "It is nothing that should concern you."

Cora pulled back, shock written on her face at the amount of anger he showed. "Sorry, I didn't think."

"You're right, remember you are a prisoner here. Watch your damn step." He snapped and pulled on a clean shirt, lacing it at the collar.

"Forgive me, I guess it slipped my mind." She ached to touch him, wanting to feel his skin on hers.

"I'll return before dawn. No more drawing circles, no more trying to be a big bad witch." He snapped as he walked out and slammed the door behind him.

Cora's heart dropped and tears threatened to spill when she heard the sound of the lock.

Darius appeared in the human world in front of Theresa's and Cora's home. Fury still filled him from when she tried to touch his scar but part of him wanted to go back and apologize for it. The thought of her fingers brushing against the harsh reminder of what mercy brought made his cock twitch and his heart speed up. He wiped a hand over his face and focused on the dwelling in front of him. The tiny dwelling didn't

———

surprise him, a small glimpse of the life magic users endured. He crossed his arms and leaned against the door of the house as his father appeared.

"Glad to see you could pull yourself away from the whore and make it here." Xavier looked over at Darius. "I do hope you are not getting too attached to her. You know that it is inevitable."

"What is?"

"Her death."

"Her life doesn't really concern me, finding out as much as I can about her life as the Gypsy Lady."

"We have all the information we need, we just need her to show her powers. Have you had any luck with playing nice?"

He shook his head. "She's let her guard down a bit, but that's all. I really don't think that she's come into her powers yet." Of course screaming at her didn't help. He recalled the look on her face and the shine in her eyes before he left. A strange pain started in his heart as he thought about her possibly crying in his room while he stood with his father.

"It's rare for them to take this long, this was the age that Aura's powers were revealed to her." Xavier strutted into the house, looking over the mess. "See anything out of the ordinary?"

Darius' eyes swept over the broken glass, shattered wood, upturned furniture, and torn linens. A shredded curtain lay in the middle of the room and he assumed it originally separated the beds, breaking the dwelling into two rooms instead of one. Coals from the fireplace trailed out, searched through by the guards, but an untouched chest in the corner remained in the disaster. "The chest, your guards missed it completely."

"Means one of the clever magic users had cast a spell on it that has since worn off. Check it, and I bet we find what we're looking for."

Darius went to it and ran his hands over the flawless wood and metal hardware. It opened easily enough and he dug through the blankets and cloaks there, pausing when his hand found the neck of a violin. He pulled it out and examined the instrument. The soft wood curved perfectly, the bridge crafted of ivory held the strings up, and though he knew she played it often not a fingerprint or a scratch showed.

"A beautiful piece, isn't it?" Xavier asked, taking it from his son. "Aura had taken good care of it, I'm glad to see that her daughter has as well."

Darius held his hand out to take it back. "Shall I see if I can use it to get her to talk more?"

"No, I have other plans for it." He laughed. "Now tell me, has she begun to trust you?"

"I already told you that she has started letting her guard down. There's really nothing more that I could ask of her." Except maybe the unthinkable. His mind drifted to thoughts of having her naked body spread under him. Her pale flesh against the black silk on his bed.

"Do not mention where you went tonight."

"Why?"

"You'll see, son. You're going to learn the fine art of having someone trust you when someone else breaks their spirit." Xavier stalked out with the violin and bow gripped in his hand.

Pounding echoing through the room woke Cora the following night. She stood in nothing but her skirts and shirt, her corset lying on the bed, when the king and guards flooded the room. Her eyes searched the faces, not finding Darius amongst them.

"Darius failed to mention to me that your appearance changes at night." Xavier's gaze raked her body and he sneered.

She clenched her fists at her side. "I wasn't aware that your son was to report everything to you."

"He is to be king one day, he must learn from me, and that means reporting to me. Grab her and bring her to the foyer," he snapped. Spinning around, his tailored coat flared around him.

The guards grabbed her and she forced herself to keep her magic down, not fighting against them. When they entered the foyer she saw the violin, leaning up against an ottoman, beckoning her to play it. She swallowed.

"Go on, pick it up. I want to hear you play. See if you are truly as good as Aura. She must have taught you when she was alive." Xavier sat down in a chair and pressed his fingers together, smiling from behind them.

Cora looked at the guards behind her and went to pick up the violin. She put the bow to the strings and gave it a long pull causing it to let out a low sound. A small smile appeared on her face as she continued her notes, playing a sad melody as she faced the king, swaying to the tune. Once the song ended she looked up at him, her stomach churned as she waited for his reaction.

"Take it from her." He pressed his lips into a thin line.

Cora snarled. "No, this is mine." She started to call on her magic and then stopped, knowing she would not win against the Demon King and the guards. She shuffled backwards, clutching the violin to her chest. Her back slammed into a wall as two of the guards reached for her, trying to pry her hands away from the violin.

"No. No." She screamed as she turned to protect it, her back against the guards.

One guard tangled his hand in her hair, using it to pull her way from the wall, while the second one secured both her arms and kept her from thrashing around.

"It's mine damn it." Tears formed at the corner of her eyes as another guard pried her fingers from the wood. She tried to yank herself out of the guard's grip to get her violin before it was handed to Xavier.

The king gave a wicked smile as he looked over the violin. "Quite the piece of work isn't it? Your mother showed it to me once. It was passed down from her mother, and then Aura passed it to you. A shame, Gypsy Lady, that it is going to end with you."

Bile rose in her throat and her body shook when the king walked over to the fire and held the violin out. The flames leapt and caught the wood of the body. She thrashed in the guards' hold, her very soul screaming out as the flame ate at the wood. Her magic flared and their hands dropped away from her as if they burned. Running, she tackled the king to the ground. Scrambling over the fallen demon she snatched the violin out of his hand. She pushed away all thoughts of not calling on her magic and held her hand over the flames. With a thought she extinguished the ones on the violin and then looked over the charred wood. Though the wood chipped off in black flecks she knew it could be repaired. She ran her fingertips over it, calling on her magic to fix what she could.

As her hand ran over the damage, images danced in her mind. Darius pulling the violin out of the chest and handing it to his father. The vision cut short when a hand wrapped around her wrist and blocked her magic.

"Tell me, you have bonds on, how did you manage magic?" Xavier snapped, ripping the violin away from her again.

Cora looked at his hand on her wrist, willing him to burst into flames. "I can only break the bonds at night." She whispered. "Darius doesn't know." In her heart she knew why she lied for Darius despite his treason. Hate grew in her for him and his part in this, but her heart craved him. Wanted him.

"You're a clever little magic user." He tossed the violin into the fire with a smirk. "I'm going to have to place stronger bonds on you." He shoved her to the guards. "Take her to the dungeon in the human world. She wouldn't survive the creatures here, and for now I

---

want her alive." He turned back to the fire watching the violin crackle as the wood burnt.

Tears streamed down her cheeks, but she felt numb as the guards pulled her out of the room, leading her out of the room.

CHAPTER SIX

The stone walls of the foyer seemed to close in on Lucas as he paced in front of the dying fire. He turned to the entrance when the hunters returned to him. "What did you find?"

"The king and the prince were there, neither of the girls were present." The first one stepped up. "That means they are both-"

"Missing, simply missing." He met the other man's eyes, the light color of the irises almost blended into the whites of his eyes in a stark contrast to the black hair pulled back tight at the base of his skull. The leather on his wrists and legs looked worn from battles and use, but in the role of a scout the normal weapons had not been added to the outfit.

"They took Cora's violin."

Lucas still remembered the precious wood and the beautiful sound the instrument made. His heart skipped a panicked beat at the thought of it being with the Demon King. "The violin, the one Aura got from her mother?"

"Yes sir."

"Alaster, find a way to get in contact with the king, he's playing dirty now, and I want my girls back."

He bowed his head. "Of course, I'll see what I can do. Shall I make a room for them here? So once we get them back they are safe?"

"You still have feelings for my daughter, don't you?" Lucas laughed a little. "Still upset that I left them in the village."

He shrugged. "Not as upset, but I want to make sure she is safe."

"She will be, both of them will be staying here."

The echoes of Cora's screams tortured Darius' ears as he ran through the dungeon looking for her. Ordered by his father to go to her. Darius couldn't believe his father put Cora through a whipping after strengthening the bonds. With the new bonds she wouldn't be able to call on any of her magic even with the help of the night.

Another scream tore through him as he found her in the main chamber, chained with her face against the wall, her back in shreds from the whip the guard wielded. Blood dripped down her back and to the floor. With another snap, she cried out as the whip split a piece of rare, untouched skin. She sobbed as her scream died out and Darius forced himself not to run to her.

"That is enough." Darius put a hand on the guard's wrist as he raised it again.

The guard dropped his arm and stepped back. "The king has sent you for her?"

"Yes, she is to return to my custody and go back to the demon realm." He walked up to her and unchained her, catching her under the arms as she fell. "I've got you." He whispered.

She snarled at him and tried to move out of his embrace. "You bastard, you knew all along what he was going to do." She drew in a breath through her clenched jaw. "He burnt my violin."

"The violin you were playing at the festival?" He asked, transporting her back to his room in the demon realm. He looked around the room, trying to decide the best action for her.

She tried to nod but cried out in pain. "Yes, my mother's violin, your father burnt it." She choked as she tried to stop the tears. Despite her effort the tiny droplets fell from her eyes. His chest ached at seeing them fall down her cheeks. "He knew it was hers, he knew how much it meant. He knows about the Gypsy Lady."

"Wait." He called out in his language and two women rushed into the room, and took the wounded witch from him.

She cringed as the women touched her and talked to each other in the same language. "What am I going to do? If my father finds out he'll kill me." She whispered and then looked at him. "And you. You knew that he was going to do it. You knew that he was going to search for the violin when you met him." Her voice seethed with anger.

Guilt formed in his gut as he watched the servants he had called. "I had no idea." His mind raced to find a way to make her believe him while his heart demanded he comfort her.

She gave a bitter laugh. "I saw it, as soon as I touched the violin. I saw you pulling it from the chest." She hissed as one of the woman pressed a warm cloth onto her wounds. She clenched her eyes shut and took a few deep breaths. "And here I thought I could trust you."

"I didn't know what he was planning on doing with it." Giving in to the need to comfort her, he sat on the bed and tried to move a piece of hair out of her face.

She dodged his touch. "He knew that it would cause me to break out my powers and prove that the bonds were no good."

"But he didn't kill you." The pain in her teary eyes pierced his heart and he turned away from her. He stood and moved to look out the window. "He only gave you stronger bonds."

"Because they aren't the powers he was expecting. The abilities I have shown are enough to prove to him that I am of Demon Hunting blood, and if I'm not mistaken those were the terms of my death."

"He wants something else. I can't put my finger on what it is though." He turned back to her.

"You're hiding things from both me and your father. You can't have divided sides. I don't understand why you keep trying to protect me."

Neither could he. When he heard of her punishment, memories of how the mounds of her breast tried to spill from her corset as she read and how the moon itself shined in her hair and eyes tangled with thoughts of how her delicate skin wouldn't be able to stand the kiss of the whip.

"Have you tried to perform magic with these new bonds?" He asked.

Cora watched as the two women left them and then turned to him. "In front of the guards that are loyal to your father? No. Besides, I'm not feeling too up for magic right now."

"As a magic user, can you not heal those wounds?" He asked, curious.

Her control over her temper impressed him as she clenched her jaw and corrected him again. "As a witch, normally I can, but that includes a large amount of energy that I don't have."

"Get some rest, lay on your side. I'll find something light to cover you with until I can find you some replacement clothes." He turned away and walked to the wardrobe.

"Do you have any whiskey?"

"I'm sorry?" He turned around, his brows drawn together.

She laughed at the look on his face. "Whiskey. A little liquor to take the edge off the pain?"

"You want to get drunk?" He turned back and found a light spread to put over her.

She smirked. "Well I hadn't planned on drinking that much, just enough to take the edge off; however, getting drunk may not be a bad idea."

The thought of a drink appealed to him as well. "I'll fetch some whiskey for you."

"Kind of you, how you treat a prisoner. Don't forget to tell your daddy that you're doing this for me. So if he finds me passed out on the bed, he knows why."

Darius shook his head as he walked out the door, chuckling to himself. Charming even in pain.

"Tell me seer, what news do you bring to me of the north kingdom?" Xavier's voice echoed off the stone walls of the seer room. Theresa tried to look up at him, the black veil she wore cast a haze over everything in front of her, but allowed her to look down into the pool.

She took a shaky breath, trying to recall the vision from earlier. "They are moving south, wishing to take the north square first, seeing that as the wealthiest part of your land. Their troops are double in numbers than ours and their weapons greater than ours."

"And do we know what makes their weapons so great?" Xavier sat up in his chair, eyes trained on her.

"They have wit-" she stopped and corrected herself, not wanting to upset Xavier, "magic users employed with their army."

"And do they have any Demon Hunters in their ranks?" His eyes flashed red as he paced in front of her.

"No sire, no one bears the mark there. The Gypsy Lady is not amongst their ranks." Theresa's voice faltered, knowing her words to be true. Tears formed in the corner of her eyes as she continued. "Because you have the Gypsy Lady in your custody."

He motioned and a guard aimed his bow and arrow at her. Xavier looked at the crone that led them. "Does she speak the truth?"

"It is how I have seen it too sire, that you have the Gypsy Lady and that the troops are moving. The evidence that there are magic users amongst the rank was shown through those controlling elements." The crone stepped up. "So she is speaking the truth, there is no arrow needed."

Xavier nodded and motioned for the arrow to be lowered. "Controlling elements is normally a Demon Hunter power."

"No sire, it's not." Theresa said. "It is an old power, true, but it is not one specially related to Demon Hunters. These magic users do not take on any quality of the element, they do not change in order to wield it."

"So what you are telling me is that the Gypsy Lady would control fire, if she was able to tap into her powers?"

The mention of Cora made the tears spill down Theresa's cheeks in silence as her heart ached for her sister. "Perhaps sire, no one really knows since she has not shown her true powers." She turned to return to her pillow.

Xavier put a hand on her shoulder to keep her from moving away from him. "One more question for you, seer. I am to receive a visitor tomorrow, a messenger that is coming from the east forest. Do you know what it pertains to?"

Theresa met his eyes through the veil. "It is a messenger from the people you have been seeking. Their leader is calling for their captives back." Joy made her heart jump at the thought of her father contacting the Demon King.

"You have grown in your powers these few nights, I am impressed. Do not harbor any hope though, I will not be giving you or your sister up." He spun away from her and stalked up the steep stairs that led out of the seer room.

The moment the door shut, Theresa ripped her veil off and threw it on the floor. "I hate that man."

"Most of us do, he is evil and cruel. He lives to make others suffer, you did well today though, by telling him the whole vision." The crone soothed.

She sighed and looked in the mirror, studying her pale face. Dark circles made their home under her eyes just from the few sleepless nights and the color blurred from the new tears trying to escape. "Except for he knows that Cora is the Gypsy Lady."

"What have I told you about worrying about her? It does you no good right now." The old woman folded the veil and put in on a shelf. "You have grown powerful in a short amount of time. I believe all you needed was to clear your mind and have proper training. Perhaps your father will see this when you meet again."

Theresa turned around. "My father? Have you seen something?"

"I have seen much, and your family and you shall reunite, but take the king's actions to heart. He is not one to let things go willingly." The crone patted Theresa's cheek. "Sleep little one, tomorrow will be a big day for you."

Two skins of whiskey in and Cora's pain started to fade. She lay on her stomach, half naked and grinning like an idiot. Darius looked over at her from his desk. The firelight flickered over her skin, coating her body in lovely shadows as she curled on her side watching him.

"Something interesting?" He turned in his chair towards her.

She gave a shrug and lowered her gaze as she felt the heat rise to her cheeks. "You," When he raised a brow she continued, "I love watching you move, the way you look like a graceful predator as you sway between objects."

"Sway? You make me sound like a dancer,

warriors aren't graceful." He laughed a little. "You're drunk, magic user."

"Witch, just say it once, without spite, without anger." A strange want uncurled in her heart, a craving to hear him say the word. "I have done nothing to you, nothing at all. Why hate me?" She met his gaze, entranced by the firelight flickering in the black irises.

He frowned, stood and walked over to her. "You're right, you haven't done anything to me, but my people-"

"That is the past, neither of us are from that generation." She pushed herself up with one arm. "Aren't you tired of hiding? Aren't you tired of pretending that you want to do what your father tells you? That past is over."

Darius' eyes wandered over her. "Maybe you're right and it is time to forget the past."

"Why, Darius, I do believe I see a little lust in your eyes." She slowly moved into a sitting position. "Is it possible for a demon to lust after a witch?" Trailing her fingertips over his cheek a new heat ran through her body different than the warmth drinking caused.

He went still. "It is not unheard of."

"Well at least you aren't claiming that it is love, cause then I'd know it was a lie." She rose up on her knees so that she was eye level with him. "But who am I to argue with feelings of lust or love?"

He laughed, one side of his mouth pulled up in a smirk. "If I didn't know any better, magic user, I'd say you were trying to seduce me."

"I'm drunk. From what I hear, it's what gypsies do when they are drunk." She leaned forward and crushed her lips to his.

He pressed a hand to the back of her head, forcing her to stay still as his tongue nudged open her lips, tangling with hers. He wrapped his fingers in her hair and pulled her away, forcing himself to let go.

Cora looked at him breathless all thoughts of him being a demon fled her mind as the room spun a little with the help of the whiskey. She wrapped her arms around his neck, pulling him down for another kiss. He gave into her and laid her back on the bed, he hesitated when her body tensed as her back touched the bed but Cora never broke the kiss. His fingers skimmed over her stomach and to the waistband of her skirt, finding the drawstring keeping it tight against the curve of her hips. He untied the knot with one hand while his lips trailed down her neck.

Her body arched to his kisses as each touch of his lips left a burning trail, adding to the flames growing in her. She closed her eyes as his hands brushed her hips and legs while he removed her skirts. A moan escaped from her partially parted lips as his hand found his way between her legs, stroking her moist core. Her breath caught as her body grew feverish for him. He continued to kiss over her collarbone, his lips finding the delicate pink bud of her right breast.

Her noises grew louder as she felt a need stir in her, his wet tongue sliding across her nipple in time with his finger stroking her core. Heat grew in her as she sat up and pushed him back, a sly smile on her face. She worked at his belt buckle, sliding his sword to the ground, examining him for a minute, and then going back to remove his pants.

"What was that look for?" He asked, running his fingers through her hair.

She chuckled and brushed her fingers down the bare skin of his thighs. "I wanted to see if you looked any less dangerous."

"And do I?" He tightened his fingers in her hair, pulling just a bit.

Her lips parted, making a strange noise somewhere between pain and pleasure. "Not at all, it's not the weapon that makes you scary."

"And what does?"

She slid her hands up his chest, untucking his shirt and then undoing the laces at the collar. "Courage, strength, talent." She pulled the shirt over his head and stepped back examining him. Her hands traced the chiseled lines of his naked chest and with each movement the moisture between her legs grew. She lowered her mouth tracing the path with her tongue. "Physically imposing helps." She whispered, "But it's not everything." She circled her tongue around his nipple.

He shivered as her teeth scraped against his skin. "You sure know how to sweet talk a man." He whispered, his fingers brushing against the bare skin of her arms.

"It isn't sweet talk. I speak of what I see." She lowered her hands, tucking a finger inside his waistband, running it around the edge. "You are a warrior inside and out."

Darius watched as his hardened cock sprung free from the confines of his pants. Cora gave it a thoughtful look before wrapping a hand around it and squeezing. His breath caught at the feel of her soft skin against his member, she began to stroke it, with careful motions she made sure it went all the way down the thick shaft an then over the large head. She looked up at him, catching his heated gaze and giving him a mischievous look before wrapping her lips around the head of his cock. Swirling her tongue around him, stroking him, she learned the taste of him and what made him shudder in pleasure. With each stroke of her tongue his member pulsed, nearly bringing him to the edge. He groaned as she took nearly the full length of his shaft into her mouth, the tip of the head hitting the back of her throat as she tried to take him completely.

Cora pulled away and looked up at him with sparkling eyes. "Like that?" She asked as she continued to move her hand over his cock.

He nodded and then pulled her up to him. "I want you. I have no idea what kind of spell you have put on me, but I want you."

"No spell, too drunk to do magic." She giggled and

kissed him, cupping his face with her hands. "All chemistry at this point. Unless you are using demon magic, then you're to blame, not me."

He deepened the kiss, trying to devour her with teeth and tongue, and then laid her back on the bed. "Okay, drunk I can deal with." He ran his hands over her naked body, "God you are beautiful."

She could feel the magic grow with every touch of his hand like a flame. She reached out and brushed his cheek. "You'll make a girl blush with talk like that."

"Maybe that is my point." He whispered against her ear, nibbling on it slightly and then kissed down her neck. "Maybe I want to give you the attention you deserve." He took a nipple into his mouth, rolling the bud on his tongue.

Cora moaned, it had been way too long since anyone caressed her this way; she squeezed her eyes shut as she felt something burn within her again. She couldn't put her finger on it. A tentative build up magic began sending tingles through her body, a hint of a warning, but it made no sense to her. Then he switched breasts and she lost all thought of magic in the pleasure of his touch.

With one thrust he entered her wet folds, the length and girth stretching her. He glided in and out of her as he moved his hips. She arched her back trying to meet his movements and push him deeper in her. Pleasure uncurled in her gut and her body ached for more. With the building pressure something flooded from her very being, flames and a need began to consume her. A feeling that had nothing to do with sex, but everything to do with power.

His thrusts sped up, and soon the pleasure devoured them both. His hot seed shot deep into her as her muscles squeezed and milked him of the precious fluid. Something strange happened when she called out his name, a red haze surrounded them and the heat building in her pushed against her very being, scalding her from the inside out. Cora tried to breathe through the mass of power, collecting it and shoving it the only place she could. With her eyes closed and in a panic, she imagined the circle she tried to invoke before and forced the power to go there. Vases shattered around them, the stone and wood creaked while the burning sensation faded, leaving a comforting warmth of performed magic.

"What was that?" Darius sat up.

"I invoked the circle, with binds on." She giggled, the alcohol still in effect.

He got out of the bed, but once he touched the circle she'd summoned he couldn't go any further. He put his hand against the invisible barrier and pulled back with a hiss, shaking his hand as if it burned. "Pull it down."

Cora sobered a bit and met his wide eyes. Though he tried to hide it, she knew the truth. "You're scared of me." She pulled her knees to her naked chest, her green eyes watching his movements "You're actually scared of me."

"You just summoned a circle from nothing, with binds on." He ran a hand through his hair. "Why does my reaction bother you so much? Fuck, we shouldn't have even done it."

Cora shook her head. "Don't worry about it." She closed her eyes and concentrated on the magic she expelled and pulled in back into her. With a physical jolt the power disappeared and Cora let out a little gasp.

Darius went to her and tried to stroke her cheek. "Cora?"

She pulled away from him. "I'm a prisoner here, remember." She snapped, flinching as the whiskey started to wear off and the pain returned in her back.

"Your powers have awakened." He whispered. "Your hair-"

"Is red like the flames, and my eyes are green and clear." She said knowing exactly what her powers waking meant. "You aren't going to be able to hide this from your father." A fine tremor started through her body, part pain and part disappointment at Darius' reaction.

He paused, his eyes searching over her. "Then we'll only have to let him see you at night. I won't let him kill you over this."

"I'm starting to think he has other plans. He had the evidence to pin me as the Gypsy Lady, why didn't he kill me then? Why go through the trouble of learning my past and my powers."

Darius stood and paced the room. "My father likes to play with his prey."

"So that's where you get it from." She snapped without realizing it. With him protecting her, she believed he wanted her, cared for her and wanted to end this war, but now she realized the stupidity of her thoughts.

He shook his head. "Don't play this game, anything I've done to protect you I've done because I wanted to, not because I'm trying to fool you."

"Oh, silly demon." She whispered. "You don't understand the extent of my powers now. I saw you conversing with your father. You not only knew about the violin, but you knew that I was dropping my guard around you." She shook her head. "I was stupid, thinking we were alike in our thoughts." She pulled the sheet around her.

He cursed under his breath. "Cora, he's a hard man to please."

"Save your excuses." She lay on her side, her back towards him, cringing as she felt blood drip from reopened wounds.

"I'll call the nurses, they should be able to help you with your pain. Without the whiskey." He stormed out the room, leaving Cora curled in a ball.

The next day the king sent for Cora and sent

———

Darius away. She was being dragged into the castle in the human realm, kicking and screaming, but she calmed when she saw Theresa kneeling next to the black carved stone seat where the king sat. The guard shoved her to her knees next to Theresa. A cry of pain escaped her lips as her knees hit the stone and pain shot through her back. There they waited.

Cora studied the floor of the foyer, trying to get the past evening out of her head when Xavier greeted a visitor the guards led in. "Welcome messenger from the east."

She recalled the way Darius' hands trailed heat as they brushed against her skin, the tenderness of his kiss when caressed her body with his lips on her body and the way they moved together in a perfect rhythm. Heat and moisture grew between her legs, and in silence she scolded herself for thinking about the man who didn't want her. Her sister's nudging brought Cora out of her daydream, forcing her to pay attention to the scene in front of her.

"The leader of the Demon Hunter pack wishes to negotiate the return of his two daughters."

Cora's head snapped up at the deep rolling male voice. Though the voice sounded different than it did in her childhood, she knew it right away. She knew Alaster as a warrior, not a typical messenger.

Xavier laughed. "So the leader has finally decided to come out of hiding."

Alaster met her gaze with a gentle smile and then turned it back to the king. "He's willing to meet, yes."

The smile warmed her and reminded her of the childhood friendship they shared years ago. Grown now, his pitch black hair fell in his light, almost white, eyes, stubble ran over his masculine jawline. If she stood him next to Darius, they would see eye to eye, with the same colored hair and the same rugged look, but with different eyes. Yet, she would still go to Darius' side instead of the other Demon Hunter. With a sigh, she tried to stop comparing the two.

The king steepled his hands in front of his mouth, thinking and then stood. "Neither of his daughters have proven useful to me, so he may have them both back." He said and then motioned with his hand. The guards shoved both girls forward. Theresa caught herself and Cora barely managed, her back screaming in pain at the sudden movements.

"Of course. Can't do much without having the correct bloodline in them." Alaster said and went to help the girls up.

Cora closed her eyes trying not to flinch at the wounds on her back pulling as the pain started to eat through her when he stood. "Alaster-"

He put a finger to her lips. "Hush, we shall speak on the way home." He helped Theresa up and led the girls out.

Cora nodded and heard Xavier call to a guard behind them, "Call for my son."

Darius sauntered into the foyer; annoyance filled him as he laid eyes on his father. "You called?"

"You've been hiding things from me again, haven't you?" Xavier stood and stalked over to his son.

"What are you talking about?"

"I could sense the changes in Cora as I sent her off with the messenger to go back to her father." Xavier raised a brow. "You knew that her powers had awakened. So tell me, how did you bring them forth?"

"I didn't, they came forth on their own after her whipping." Darius' mind raced as he tried to figure out why his father would send Cora away. A strange pain started in his chest at the thought of never seeing Cora again, never being able to run his fingers through her red hair, to taste her sweet lips. At those thoughts, his body ached to hold her and his heart wished to chase after her.

"Do not lie to me, son." Xavier laughed. "You are starting to care for the little whore. You need to forget about her; she is just another pawn in my plan. The tribe to the north is moving in on us, it is rumored that they have magic users in their ranks."

The news made Darius start. "I'm sorry, did you say in their ranks? As in fighting along side of their soldiers?"

"Yes, they have apparently allied with them." Xavier said, "it is a smart move."

"If they can control them, yes, but magic users aren't easily controlled as we know." His mind traveled to Cora, "especially when they have a mind of their own."

"You'll see your precious magic user again, do not fear my son." Xavier smiled and walked out. "Prepare for battle, there will be a bloody one ahead of us."

"It's a trap, you know." Theresa whispered as they walked through the woods. "They are using us to get to Father."

"Oh I'm sure of that. Besides why do you think he sent a warrior instead of a messenger? He was expecting problems." Alaster glanced back at Cora as she stumbled over another tree root. "Are you doing all right?"

Despite the loose peasant shirt and the bandages the pain started to wear on her. "I'm fine, let's just get home." She didn't want to face her father, not after so many years. The anger and fear curled tight in her stomach at every reaction she thought he might have. Her limbs seemed to be growing heavy as she followed the other two through the forest, part from the pain and part from the lack of desire to move forward. This time a pesky rock caught her shoe and she tumbled towards the ground.

Theresa caught her, "Careful, Cora."

"Sorry." She grumbled, and Alaster sighed.

"I didn't think to bring other horses, and none of us are talented enough to create a door."

"Well, not exactly," Cora sighed. She walked over to a tree and laid her hand on it, mumbling a spell she had heard only a few times as a child. The wind swirled around them, swirling as a glow spread from Cora's hand and formed an glowing yellow arch on the tree.

She stepped back and then looked at the wide and questioning eyes of the other two. "Don't ask questions, I'm not dealing with them right now." She walked through, shivering as the magic caused the little hairs on her neck to stand up. She took in the ridged, dark walls of stone and dirt. The damp air clung to her lungs and sent chills through her, causing her to wrap her arms around herself.

Alaster walked through next, followed by Theresa. Theresa brushed her arms as if trying to get the magic off her and Alaster started to speak, but Cora cut him off.

"I need to see a healer." She started down one of the man made halls.

Alaster took a few quick steps to catch up to her. "Let me get you and Theresa settled in your rooms. You shouldn't be up and walking around right now."

"Fine." Anything to put off seeing her father. She turned Theresa, "Are you harmed?"

Theresa shook her head. "I'm fine, I wasn't in danger as long as I gave him the correct information with the visions."

"You told him about the violin." The assumption brought on a new wave of anger and Cora clenched her fists, trying not to lash out. "You told him who I was."

Theresa paused and her features paled. "The violin was concealed with a spell in the chest. They found it?"

"And threw it in a fire." She turned back and continued walking. Alaster put a hand on the small of her back and she flinched away from him. "Don't touch me." She found tears stinging at the corner of her eyes at the memory of losing her violin.

Theresa shook her head and went to her sister's side. "I didn't tell them, I hid it when they raided the house."

"It doesn't matter now." Alaster said, stopping in front of two doorways covered with tan fabric hung from bars. "Theresa this is your room. Cora will be staying right next door."

Theresa nodded and turned away from Cora. "I'll see you later."

"I will come see you once I'm healed." She said.

"After you speak to your father." Alaster whispered.

Cora sneered. "After I show Father that he was wrong about me." She met Theresa's eyes, "Want me to come get you before that, you may be the only thing to keep him calm."

She gave a shaky laugh. "I may come with you. I hope you get those wounds taken care of." She walked into her room and pulled the curtain across the entry.

Alaster led Cora a few yards away and moved the curtain aside for her room. "Here you go. May I see your back?"

"Since when were you a healer? I thought you were a warrior, of course apparently you wear many hats." She looked around the room. A small mattress lay on the floor with a fur blanket folded on it. No windows to let light in because of the nature of the dwelling, but she didn't care. "Not really much."

Alaster frowned. "Better than what you did have, at least here you are safe."

"Ah yes, safe, cause that is what truly matters now that my powers have come out." She shook her head and then slipped her shirt over her head, letting out a whimper as she pulled on the wound. "We'll need to replace the bandages if you can't heal the damage."

Alaster sighed and manifested a stool for her to sit

on. "Sit down. I should be able to heal the damage. What on earth did you do to deserve a whipping?"

"I was a prisoner there, truly I didn't have to do anything to deserve it; however, I attacked the king when he threw my violin into the fire. The violin I had trusted Theresa to keep safe." She sat and started to unwrap the bandages.

He took the edge of the bandage from her and started to unwrap her himself. "Go easy on Theresa, this journey hasn't been easy on her either."

"Oh of course. She has been trained to use her powers instead of having them bound." She held up her wrists.

"Funny that you bring that up, how are you able to perform magic with the bindings on?" He examined her back after moving her hair over her shoulder. "You're lucky these aren't infected."

Cora glanced over her shoulder at him. "My demon hunting blood awoke in me, apparently that is not a bloodline that the binds work on."

"Your father wants to see you once you are up to visiting."

"I will be after you finish up with the wounds. I'm eager to talk to him about how he lied to me all my life." The sarcasm sounded through her voice and she clenched her jaw as he put his hand against her back.

"Everything that he's done has been for a reason."

She took even breaths as she felt his magic touch her and mix in order to heal the wounds there. The skin knit itself back together, making no noise, causing no pain, and leaving no marks. The though of having no scars from the experience made her mind wander to Darius' back and the scar he bore. She remembered him flinching when she touched it, the regret she saw in his eyes.

"Cora?" Alaster stroked her hair as he pulled it away from her shoulder. "How do you feel?"

She blinked a few times and then turned towards

---

him. "Better." She pulled her shirt over her head. "Let's get my sister and go visit Father, shall we?"

"I am not welcomed in the conference, just you and your sister." He smiled and stroked her cheek. "I will see you after."

At one time Cora would have loved his attention, but now his hand just felt warm against her skin. No tingles spread from him, nothing stirred her body and she knew why. She wanted Darius. She stepped away, "Then I shall get Theresa and head to see him."

"I will lead the way for you, you are still new to these caverns." He let his hand drop back to his side. "Something is bothering you."

Cora gave a bitter laugh. "Something that you'll never understand Alaster. Let me get settled here and find out what my father plans for me, before you start trying to court me."

He bowed his head and moved the curtain aside for her. She ducked under his arm and walked the few yards down to Theresa's room. "Sister of mine?"

"Healed already?" Theresa asked, sticking her head around the curtain.

Cora held her arms out and spun around. "Almost as good as new."

"Almost, but I like the new improvement. I can't believe you came into your powers." Theresa took her sister's hand as Alaster started walking down the tunnel.

Cora shrugged. "What can I say? Apparently being pushed too far was all I needed." She refused to share what it took. A shiver crawled over her body as she recalled the soft caress of Darius' hands over her skin.

"You sure you're alright?" Alaster asked, glancing back at her.

Theresa squeezed her hand. "She's fine, she's just got a lot to recover from and a lot to take in. You have to remember this is the first time that she will have seen our father since he left us in the village."

"Yes." Cora agreed, not wanting to share all the thoughts on her mind.

Alaster bowed his head slightly in acknowledgment. "Forgive me, Lucas waits behind those doors." He motioned to the only room with two great wooden doors covering the entrance.

Cora reached forward and pulled one open, waltzing right in without hesitation. She would face this head on and use her hate and anger to her advantage. A smirk crossed her face as she saw her father standing in front of the fire, his hazel eyes trained on her. "Daddy, I'm home."

CHAPTER SEVEN

"Cora, my child, it's good to finally see you." Lucas reached for her hand.

She stepped away from him. "Don't forget traditions, you are to greet the eldest child first." Cora motioned to Theresa. "If not for her you would have no younger daughter. Remember that. Respect that." Cora made sure the anger sounded in her voice.

Lucas sneered before pulling Theresa into a hug. "Forgive me, Cora is right. I have much to thank you for."

"Thank you, father, but truly Cora took better care of me than I did her." Theresa wrapped her arms around him, squeezing him tight.

Jealousy filled Cora, and she spoke sharper than she meant to. "Alaster said that you wanted to see us."

Lucas pulled away from Theresa and nodded. "I wanted to see if what he said was true, which I see indeed that it is. Here stands my daughter, a true Demon Hunter."

"Which you thought was impossible so you abandoned me." Cora said.

"You don't understand the circumstances that surrounded the situation." Lucas ran a hand through his graying hair.

Of course he would think that. "Like my mother being killed by the Demon King?" She tilted her head. "Or like the fact that you've been keeping in contact with Theresa. Or how you knew that I was showing signs and still left us in the village."

He looked at Theresa, his eyebrows raised. "Yes, Xavier killed your mother. He thought that the Gypsy Lady was his little pet, someone to perform only for him in every way. He dealt with the masks, the charades, everything because he thought it meant that she was inferior to him. He didn't know it was because she was a Demon Hunter."

"So when did you meet her, since when did you tolerate infidelity?" Cora moved in front of the fire and took a seat. "Come father, why don't we talk and catch up about this?"

His eyes flickered to Theresa. "You should go visit your mother."

"Do not try to change subjects. I deserve to know." Theresa narrowed her eyes, and then strolled over to sit with Cora.

Lucas summoned a chair for himself and sat in front of the girls, "Theresa's mother was away on her own mission. Aura came to me because she feared the Demon King. This was before he had totally taken over the village, before he started moving his influences further through the land. He had already made the vow to kill all Demon Hunters that he came in contact with, claiming that he had his reasons to." He ran a hand through his hair and then looked at Cora.

"We had an affair, neither of us were proud of it, and the next thing I knew she disappeared for nine months. I was worried about what the Demon King had done to her, but Xavier was looking for her as well, and the people were losing hope because the Gypsy Lady had disappeared. One night, I heard her violin playing by the river, a tune that would haunt me forever. I found her by the river with a bundle at her feet. When I approached her, she gave me you. She would visit and bring things for you while Elsie and I lived together in the village."

"You didn't love her." Cora said, "That's why you and Ellie were always resentful towards me. Ellie didn't want to believe that I came from another woman. She could see it in my looks, despite how much she wanted to love me as her own. I look more like my mother." Cora shook her head. "Xavier found her again, six years later and killed her. On that same river bed that you found me with her."

He frowned. "You remember the night that I came to tell you that?"

"I was five, of course I do. It was always the highlight of my month when she would visit, and then you came home to tell me that she would not longer come. You didn't tell me that she was killed. I had to learn that from the Demon King himself." The anger grew in Cora. "You have hidden too much from me."

His face remained blank, and Cora wondered if he felt any guilt at all. "Only because it was needed, had you possessed information on us then the Demon King would have tortured you until he was able to get the information."

"Or until my powers came out, because his grand plan was to kill me, until he realized that he could use me to get to you and now all the hunters are in danger." She said.

A strange smile crossed his face. "No, we aren't, we have grown in numbers and now we can hold our own against him. We have joined with the village in the north and plan on marching with them, especially now that you have joined our ranks."

"You were the cloaked figure that I saw at the head of the army." Theresa gasped, a hand to her

---

mouth. "You can't lead that attack. The king knows you are coming."

"How?"

"Remember your other daughter is a seer, the king is a master at using everything to his advantage. Theresa saw the attack," Cora said.

"But she is untrained."

Cora looked at Theresa and raised a brow. "It looks like he's been purposely keeping you weakened as well." She turned back to him. "She was being trained by the kings oracles and had no choice but to tell the king what she saw. So you've screwed yourself over unless you can find another plan of attack."

He met eyes with Cora. "You're our ticket in. He'll want you back, especially now that you've met with me."

"I'm not going to be your pawn." She crossed her arms. "I just got out of their realm, I have no desire to go back in there." Darius came to mind and her heart ached to see him again, but she doubted he wanted to see her. She shook her head, clearing the thoughts from her mind. "The answer is no."

Lucas looked at Theresa and motioned to Cora. "Can you talk sense into her?"

"She's a big girl that can answer for herself." Theresa said.

He sighed. "Fine you don't want to help in the battle, then you both will be staying here- sheltered."

Cora stood. "I suppose that is fair. I don't really think attacking him is a good idea, especially if he knows you are coming. It probably means that he knows you've joined the north village."

"You really think that his oracles are that good?" Lucas laughed. "You put too much faith in those creatures."

Theresa shook her head. "Here's the funny thing, the oracles are all descendants of Demon Hunters, just like me."

"You're kidding right?" He frowned. "We thought

they simply killed all Demon Hunter children when they could."

"It's amazing how much neither culture knows about the other." Cora said.

"Are you insinuating that they are just as naïve about us? Stop buying into their lies."

Cora shrugged. "As usual, you belittle your daughter. I am going to rest, and see if I can't get my hands on a new deck of cards, or maybe a scrying mirror." She spun to leave the room, neither Theresa or Lucas made a move to stop her.

Theresa sighed as the door closed behind Cora. "She has not been the same since we have left the demon realm."

"And you are?" Lucas asked. "You have grown much stronger as well. I would think that both of you would be happy with the changes."

"So I was trained how to use my powers to their advantages. Why should I be happy with that?"

"Because now you can use it to help us." He put a hand on her shoulder. "Even if you're not on the field you'll be a great help to us all."

A pang of disgust ran through her as she realized her father wanted to use her too. "As soon as I can see them." She glanced at the door, wondering if the sick feeling sliding through her was what Cora felt. "Do not push Cora, she really has no interest in being on the field. She's still recovering from being with them and her violin being burnt."

Lucas froze. "Aura's violin."

"Yes, the one thing that she had that tied her to her mother and now it's gone." Theresa said. "I don't know how he got it, because I had it concealed, but I know that watching it burn nearly killed her."

"And I'm assuming that had something to do with her powers being brought out. Now she has to be trained as one of us, she doesn't really have a choice in the matter. The blood and the power are there."

"I don't think she'll let you use her against the Demon king." Theresa laughed. "She's too smart for that. The only things she wanted in her life were not to be used and to not have to hide."

"Neither which are logical in this day and age. She will be under the command of the general. It is up to him"

"If she decides to march with you."

"I don't think you understand, there is no choice for her now. There are terms she must follow as one of us."

Theresa bit her lip as she tried to think of a way to keep Cora off the field. She recalled the vision of death from days before and an ache grew in her, urging her on to keep it from coming true. "She won't be trained in time for her to march with you."

Lucas remained silent for a moment, stroking his chin in thought. "And she wouldn't have to if we used her as bait. We could put her back in the village, let her continue as the Gypsy Lady."

"I thought you wanted to protect your daughter, but that's putting her back in danger. The safest place for her would be here."

"But her presence in the village would be much more productive. Don't you see, we need to show the Demon King that he hasn't won!" He said, "I think it would be best for you two to return to the village."

She threw her arms up in the exasperation. "You're impossible to deal with. You only think about how you could use her."

"That's not completely true." He looked at the fire. "I was thrilled when Aura brought her to me, because I knew Aura's blood line was strong and that Cora could be a Demon Hunter, but then I realized that she had been sleeping with a demon." He gave a bitter laugh. "I couldn't figure out what she was thinking. Such vile creatures they are and to think that Cora could have been his child." He shook his head. "To think that demons and witches could breed together."

With a sigh Theresa went to the bookshelf near the fireplace. "You know the history of the Gypsy Lady." She pulled a book from the shelf. "So it shouldn't surprise you, and you know history repeats itself. So maybe we should all study up." She handed him the book.

"What are you hinting at, what have you seen?"

She shook her head. "Nothing, I'm just tired of everyone not being able to think for themselves."

"It seems to me that you and your sister have a lot to recover from." He put the book back on the shelf. "Why don't you go rest while I figure out how to get you back to the village." He said, his voice soothing as if he spoke to a small child.

Theresa let out an impatient sigh as she walked out of the room. She knew her father to be stubborn, but she couldn't comprehend what his thoughts were. Anger led to a growl of frustration as she thought about going back to the village where neither sister would be safe. She looked up to see Alaster leaning against the wall, his face set with a frown. "What's wrong now?" She asked, crossing her arms.

"Your sister just kicked me out of her room when I was trying to talk to her. Silly me, I thought that she and I could get along now that we're adults."

"Good luck with that. She's in a mood thanks to our father."

"Lovely." Alaster ran his fingers through his hair. "So I guess asking her if she wants to go star gazing is probably out of the question?"

Theresa turned away, her brows raised and a small smile on her face. "I think she'd be shocked that you asked, and might actually go with you." A relaxing night out of the caverns may be what Cora needed?

"You really think so? I mean, I know she likes that kind of thing, but she's upset and-"

Theresa pushed him towards Cora's room. "Go talk to her, get her to relax some. And whatever you do, don't mention the violin."

He nodded and then went back to Cora's room, knocking on the stone next to the curtain he called out. "Cora?"

Alaster's voice sounded far away as Cora's own words and thoughts dripped from her lips. *"The demons will be knocked back and the hunters will return to their former glory."* Her eyes focused on the mirror in front of her, the reflection of the candle in the human realm flickering in the glass behind her, allowing her to see the scene. An army of hunters moving towards the castle, at the head of it her father.

She didn't flinch when she heard someone enter the room, the vision in front of her changing. Standing next to Darius, she saw herself holding her mask in one hand and a new violin in the other. Darius clutched a sword, blood dripping from the blade. *"They will return, rise up in power with the help of the demons, there will be no return for the Gypsy Lady, but there will be no need."* Her lips barely moved as the words fell from them. *"The reign of the Demon King is over and the people will no longer live in fear. The king of swords will right the injustice and take the Gypsy Lady as his own."*

Cora's words fell silent as she watched the scene in the mirror shift again, the Demon King stood in the middle of a room, a broken body lay dying in front of him. Brown hair covered the victim's face, the slim veil of the seer cast to the side and arrows skewered the body.

"A sacrifice is required to let lose the true hunter, to allow the magic to pass flawlessly through the binds." She tilted her head to the side. "A blood sacrifice of family and faith. Of protection and trust."

Blinking a few times the images faded and she shook her head, trying to make sense of it all. The

---

visions left her with a sense of panic climbing through her, something she should be freaking out about and trying to change. Alaster chose that moment to step away from the wall. "I'm impressed, it seems to me that your skills have surpassed your sister's."

At the mention of Theresa, Cora froze, the image in the glass becoming clear, the seer's veil, the brown hair, the dress, blood, and family. "No, no, no." She stood, knocking over the candle, flame disappearing with a whiff of smoke. "This can't be happening. She can't die." A thread of panic exploded in her and she raced for the door.

Alaster caught her around the waist to keep her from exiting. "Theresa is safe, just like you here in the walls of our home. Cora, you're pale, what's wrong?"

She tore away from him and met his gaze, fighting the tears gathering. "I saw Theresa dying. She's going to be killed at the hands of the Demon King."

"The blood sacrifice that you had talked about. Don't worry, there is time to change all this."

"Spoken like someone who isn't a seer." She grumbled and looked down at the bonds still on her wrists. "I need to find a welder or a metal worker to get these off me. " She sighed and rubbed her eyes.

He seemed to hesitate, reaching out to touch the bands and then stopping short. "I'll see what I can do for them tomorrow. For now, why don't you join me for a walk outside?"

She raised a brow. "No one else ever wants to walk in the dark. You know the old stories about the demons coming to get you."

He laughed. "You don't truly believe that, and I like the night sky. I want to go stargazing."

Needing the distraction from the visions, she wanted to go. "Alright, I'll allow you to walk with me outside this once, but don't make a habit of it." She grabbed a cloak that was on her bed. "Don't tell my father."

He led her into the hall, remaining silent until they exited the maze of caverns and in the forest. "I know a great clearing, follow me." He held his hand out to her.

She looked at the hand and frowned at the unfamiliar gesture and attention. She took his hand with hesitation and let him lead her.

"You think your father would have a fit if you were out here?" His steps never hesitated as he walked through the overgrown forest.

"He wants me to be well rested for when he returns me back to the village." She took her time following his steps, trusting he knew the way.

"Why would he do that, the safest place for you now is with us, with the clan." He looked back at her, and then moved some bushes out of the way for her to pass.

She gave a bitter laugh. "To use me as bait."

"He plans on baiting the king with you." His eyes widened. "Your own father."

She shrugged and then looked up at the sky. "He's not much of a father. I don't expect anything else from him. First and foremost he's always been a soldier."

"That doesn't bother you at all?" Alaster sat down on a fallen log.

She smiled, her body relaxed under the blanket of stars. "No. I've lived without him most my life, I don't need him to save me now."

The wind carried her scent towards him; Darius closed his red eyes as he inhaled the sweet smell. The need to ensure her safety had filled him the moment she left. He wanted to make sure her warrior of a father hadn't done something stupid. His leathery, bat-like, demon wings cut through the air without a sound as he went in search of the woman who stole his heart.

He followed her scent and landed outside the

clearing, using the shadows to hide himself from view. Through the trees he could see her, looking up at the sky studying the stars above her, her hand limp in the man's grasp. Darius tried not to snarl at the male touching his witch. With a shake of his head, he tried to derail the thought and remind himself she didn't belong to him. He had abandoned her in fear after they slept together. At the memory of the look in her eyes and his heart pounded and ached, reminding him of how he screwed up. Turning back to the scene at hand, the serene look on her face calmed him. Despite the short amount of time she had to recover, her body seemed relaxed, as if no wounds marred her toned back. Her hand slipped from the male's as she pointed to the sky, showing him different constellations. The man next to her looked familiar, but he pushed the thought away, focusing only on the fact that another man was touching her. Darius took a few steps closer to hear her voice, wanting it to be him standing under the stars with her. His clawed foot snapped a twig and he froze as the sound echoed through the clearing and the couple looked towards where he stood.

"What was that?" Alaster stood from his stump and went to draw his sword.

Cora put her hand on top of his, staying his sword. She spotted the red eyes and knew who stood in the forest watching them. "Don't worry about it, just a creature passing by. It means us no harm."

"Are you sure? I thought I saw red eyes." Alaster moved in front of her and she rolled her eyes. "If there is a demon out there it means that he was able to follow us, and they'll follow us back home."

Cora shook her head. "No one in this night except you and I, the eyes you saw belonged to that of a bat." She whispered. "Don't let the wildlife spook you."

"We should head back either way. Your father will

have my head if he discovers you are gone." His hand fell away from his hilt. "And I don't really want to ruin my chances with you."

His words surprised her, but she shook her head. "Go on home, I'll be there soon. I'll draw a door to get me home safely."

"I don-"

"You want to have a chance with me, then you must allow me my freedom. Now go." She gave him a gentle smile, hoping he believed her.

He kissed her cheek. "Please come see me when you get back so I know that you're safe."

"I will and if not in person, I will send a servant to tell you." She bowed her head and watched Alaster run off like a frightened rabbit into the night and towards the cave. Cora kept her back turned to Darius as he stepped into the clearing.

"Brave of you to trust me so much." His voice became a deep snarl in this form.

She turned and looked him over; he reminded her much of the images in the book she read. He towered over her, the moon casting shadows on the dark skin and leather wings tucked against his back. The claw-like hands kept him from forming a fist, but looked like lethal weapons while his elongated feet with talon-like toes dug into the ground with impatience. "Stupid of me to trust you, but I sense that you aren't here to harm me. Are you here to ask for my aid as well?"

"I came to make sure that you were safe, I had no idea what to expect when my father said that you were gone." Darius went to touch her face, but let his arm fall to his side. "I hate to admit that I miss your company."

She gave a soft laugh, wanting to believe his words. "You miss my body in your bed already. I won't become your servant and I won't be your prisoner." The thought of him turning away from her again made anger crawl through her.

"What about my lover?"

"You mean your whore? I hear demons like to shower their whores with pretty things, and keep them much like harlots, or is that only your father?" She narrowed her eyes. "What are you doing here, Darius?"

He took a deep breath and pulled his other form into himself, the more human part of him emerging in front of her. "I mean what I say, I came to make sure you were safe. I did not mean to interrupt the courting session."

"Alaster means well, but he'll never have my heart." She toyed with the tie of her cloak. "I never really wanted a Demon Hunter as a mate, it means that I would risk my children having to either be a hunter or hide any blood relation they had to me. Having gone through life like that, I can't imagine bringing a child into that."

"He cares for you, you can tell by the way he wanted to protect you from me. Why didn't you let him attack me?"

She gave a soft laugh. "So you could kill him? And my father would get to rub in my face how dangerous it was to be out here?"

"Your father sounds like an overprotective guy." Darius ran a hand down her cheek. "How would he feel about us?"

She pulled away, blushing and looking down. "There is no us, it was one night while I was drunk and in pain. Witches and demons can't be together, remember? You freaked out because I accidentally locked you in a circle." His touch calmed her anger when she didn't want it.

"I'm sorry." He cupped her chin and kissed her. "I guess I have to leave you to your world. There is a war coming and I don't know the next chance I'll get to see you." In an instant he took on his demon form and shot to the sky.

Once recovered from the kiss, Cora sighed and approached a tree to summon a door. Her heart heavy, nothing made sense to her and the visions clouded her mind. She knew the demon had captured her heart. Reasoning told her she would be killed for her treason when the Demon Hunters found out, but still she craved him.

She put her hand up and summoned the door, walking through it, she looked around her new room and wept. She closed her eyes and took a moment to settle her heart and tears, before going to find Alaster.

"You have no idea what you're talking about. Cora is perfectly capable of living in the village. She lived there for years, escaping guards and dodging the king." Lucas looked at the soldier in front of him. "I'm sorry that you fancy her, but that is not going to change the part that she plays in this war."

Alaster's brows cinched together. "I don't think you understand, you are putting an innocent life on the line."

"The moment those powers came through she was no longer innocent. She has a part to play just like everyone else." Lucas snapped. "I will schedule her training for certain days and others she will make her appearance as the Gypsy Lady, so that the people will know that we have not lost."

"Not yet at least. Until they see her executed in public." Alaster growled. "Is that what you want? Your daughter's blood staining the cobblestones of the village?"

Lucas paused at that, his mind spinning. Visions eluded him as if the goddess decided to wipe clean his powers and give them to his daughters. "Have you seen something, or have either of the girls mentioned it?"

"No, but you know that is what will happen if the king gets his hands on her. He will kill her just to make a point to the people. I'm sure that seeing her has brought up some bad memories for him as well. There was a rumor that he loved the Gypsy Lady, and that's why he tried to keep her to himself."

Lucas laughed. "Yes, I'm sure that was it. He didn't have enough women already in his harem. Cora is clever enough not be caught, and strong enough to escape now. The fact that she can do magic with the bands on proves that."

"But she is still merely a woman, weakened by what her heart wants and what her mind is telling her she needs to do. You want her to be thinking of freedom in battle?"

Cora stepped in and cleared her throat. "I will not be in the battle, but I would like to return to the village."

Lucas smiled and looked at her. "I knew you would come around."

"I don't belong here and you've made it quite clear that you don't want me here. Return me to the village, but keep Theresa here so that she will remain safe."

"You don't want her with you? What has gotten into you?"

"I have seen a vision of Theresa dying. I know that it would break your heart and Elsie's heart, so you must keep her safe, because I will not be responsible for her death." She said.

"A bargain then, you return to the village and act as bait and I will keep Theresa here."

Alaster shook his head. "That is trading one life for another, how is that a good idea?"

Cora held up a hand and Lucas felt a spark of pride. "Remember what I said Alaster, I need to be allowed my freedom. I do think that it would be a wise idea to have more Demon Hunters in the village. It would bring a bigger presence and help your allies have more confidence in you. You don't want them to think that you are holding back all your men."

"She speaks the truth. I will volunteer to lead a group of men in the village. We will establish ourselves and lay low until we are needed to aid the village from the north." He glanced at Cora and then Lucas.

Cora turned her calm eyes to Lucas'. "The warriors there would also attract the king. So if you want to get his attention, that would be the way."

"So be it, Alaster, I trust you to get a team together to move to the village. Cora will be going there tomorrow night so that she can use the cover of the night to move back to her dwelling." He turned his back to them.

Cora walked out of the room, her body tense as Alaster followed her.

"I see you returned safe." He whispered.

Cora gave a bitter laugh. "Yes, to see you trying to convince my father not to send me out. What is wrong with you?"

"I was trying to help."

"And you're going to get yourself killed. You haven't seen the Demon King, his magic is insane and unpredictable." She stormed off to her room and paused outside the curtain. "He's sending you on a suicide mission."

"You don't truly believe that. He wouldn't send his own daughter on a mission like that. He wants to have you trained in your abilities." He shook his head.

"I don't think you understand. He's only training me so that I can hold my own in a battle, to give his people and the people of the northern village a chance to attack the king." She sighed. "I'm going to go say good night to Theresa. I will speak with you tomorrow about moving back to the village."

Alaster kissed her cheek. "Sleep well." He walked off, his shoulders slumped.

Cora wiped her cheek off and walked down the hall to Theresa's room. "You asleep?"

"No, I was waiting to see how your date went." Theresa closed the book sitting in her lap.

"It wasn't a date, it was an excuse to get out of here." Cora shrugged and went to sit by her "It went fine until he freaked out about an animal in the woods. He thought it was a demon."

"He's paranoid." Theresa glared at her, reading her thoughts. "You didn't just come here to say goodnight."

Damn her skills. "No, Father is sending me to the village while you stay here and hone your skills."

"I don't like it."

"I know, but there will be guards. I don't think the king will be stupid enough to attack the village, and I don't think it is me that he is after." Cora folded her hands. "So I think everything will be fine. Besides, if you stay here then you can learn more."

Theresa shook her head. "And what about you? What about your powers?"

"I will be trained when I live there, but I also have to walk around as the Gypsy Lady, to give the people hope again." She said with conviction. "That's one thing I don't mind."

"You don't have the violin anymore, how are you going to entrance them?" Theresa snapped. "The Demon King took that way."

Cora cringed as she remembered the smell of the fire burning, the crisp burnt wood and the sound of the strings breaking. "I'll figure something out. I had other talents as the Gypsy."

"You can't read for everyone in that village, there are those who would turn you in." Theresa let out a frustrated sigh.

"A risk that I'm sure Father would be glad to see." Cora pulled her sister into a hug. "Don't worry about me. Take care of yourself for once, and take advantage of what is being offered. I need you here to tell me what is going on inside here, where I won't be able to hear or see, where I'm not truly welcomed."

"Okay, I guess. When you put it like that it makes a lot of sense." Theresa wrapped her arms around her. "I love you and don't get yourself killed or captured."

"I will try my hardest."

CHAPTER EIGHT

Cora looked around their house; even with everything still in shambles, she smiled. With no need to hide her magic any more she waved a hand and watched as everything went back into the proper places. She gave a sigh of relief and then her look saddened as she saw an empty spot where her violin used to hide.

"Don't mourn over it too long, we'll have another one crafted for you." Alaster's gentle voice came from behind her.

She couldn't help but wonder what he meant by 'we'. Certainly he didn't think they were together. "I can order one myself. I should have a little bit of money stashed somewhere from my jobs. If not, then I can earn enough for a new violin with a couple rich clients who are easy to please when it comes to magic."

"You're not a magic whore anymore."

Cora spun around, anger coursing through her.

Alaster paled. "That's not what I-"

"Yes it is, you think that's why I performed magic? So I could be a whore and earn money? There were plenty of other ways to earn money in the city. I

94

performed magic because I needed to, because I felt like it was taking my body, my life." She yelled in his face. "If you think that I was simply whoring myself out for the money, then march your ass out of my home."

His mouth opened and closed a couple times as he struggled to find the right words. "I'm sorry." He finally sputtered out.

She closed her eyes. "Right. Again, don't worry about the violin, I'll get another one crafted." She took her cloak off and hung it near the fireplace. Imagining a fire burning in the fireplace, she closed her eyes and held her hand out. Within seconds the flames started to dance up between the logs that had been left there.

Alaster stepped up next to her, "That's amazing, really, who would have thought that you would have such control after first coming into your powers."

"I'm just lucky I guess, from what I hear it's in the blood line. Hopefully the control will increase with time." She looked around. "Everything is in order. I'm assuming that you found a place to stay, as well as places for the others?"

He nodded. "I'm just a few doors down from you and the others are scattered around the city."

"Good, I'll be going out tonight as the Gypsy Lady, just to walk the shores. Do not follow me or you'll tip people off as to what is going on."

"I don't like the thought of you alone out there."

She laughed. "You didn't listen very well when my father told you that I've managed to live on my own out here before. I can avoid the guards, charm the city, and maybe make some money doing parlor tricks. I'm safer here than I am in the forest, or in the caverns."

"As you wish, but if there is any trouble, I want to know about it. Please." He met her eyes and took her hands. "I worry about you."

Cora granted him a kiss on the cheek. "And I appreciate it, but I don't need anyone to worry over me."

"Fine, just stay safe." He laughed and left.

She nodded. Stay safe. She would do her best, she knew exactly where she would go tonight. She hadn't lied when she said the bank, but she'd be going to the same creature her mother went to for a violin. She waited until she knew Alaster would be tucked away in his dwelling, taking her time to change into her skirts, corset and mask. A cloak completed her outfit as she made her way into the night.

No one traveled along the cobblestone roads, no horses' hooves sounded through the darkness, no shoes shuffled under the nearly new moon. Cast in silence and shadows the night would provide perfect cover for going to the river. She pulled her hood up and took a trail to the old docks, the one the boatmen rarely used for sake of safety with exception of one who checked the dock often.

Watching her step she made her way to the edge of the dock, her feet navigating through the rotten wood to find only the good steps. She smiled as she saw the boat coming from the shadows. She could hear the old boat man singing as he approached her.

"Being down here tonight, Gypsy Lady, must mean you want something. No one comes to see Leon here anymore."

Cora bowed her head. "You are right, I have come seeking something. Years ago, you made a violin for me."

"Ah yes, when you were a young sprite," he said with a gleam in his eye. "Your violin had been destroyed, you were pregnant with child. You wanted another one, just like the Gypsy Lady before you." He chuckled when she tensed. "Yes, I know that you are not the same woman, but you are safe with me."

"What do you want in exchange for the violin?" She fussed with her skirts, wondering about the boatman's nature.

He smiled at her. "I will not send the hellhound

after you, not for your soul, it is too precious to leave this world. I want you to end the war, so that creatures can walk as they were meant to. Amongst each other."

"How do you expect me to do that?" She asked, her mind flashing to something, a fleeting vision of a ceremony.

He bowed his head. "Tis fate, and you will still walk the night as the Gypsy Lady, showing no fear of the demons, working side by side with them." He tilted his head and then held his hand out. "Come with me, and we shall get you a new violin that will sing of your praises and complement your beauty." He held his slim hand out to her.

Cora took his hand and stepped into the boat. Noticing the lack of rocking, she glanced at Leon and smiled. "Where to, ferryman?"

"To the depths of the city that you have not seen before, where the creatures of the past dwell in safe shelter away from the Demon King." He started to move the boat back into the shadows, south in the river stream.

Cora looked around as the gray stone took on a darker shade and green moss started climbing the walls. No light to signal the end of the tunnel as Leon continued into the darkness.

"Gypsy you are sworn to keep this place secret and if you are to visit without one of us you will be instantly killed. Understood?" His voice almost fell to a snarl with his threat.

She bowed her head. "I understand. I am honored that you trust me with such a secret."

"You have trusted me with yours for years, it is only fair that I return the favor." He laughed as she started to speak. "Even if you did not know that you were trusting me. Your mother trusted me as well, and her mother before that. Though I find your heritage interesting, most gypsy ladies are born from demon and witch blood, not Demon Hunter blood."

She frowned. "My mother is where my demon hunting blood comes from."

"Ah, yes, but any demon blood mixed with a witch is what creates that blood." As Leon looked up at her his eyes glazed over. "Fate has such special plans for you." He stopped at a dock and got out of the boat, holding a slim hand to her. "We walk from here."

Still in the depths of the tunnel, Cora suspected they were further underground, and no longer on the surface of the village. She took his hand and let him help her from the boat. "Where are we?" The damp air made her shiver even with the cloak pulled around her, and yet something comforted her.

"We call it home, others call it hell, but you know that this is not the same hell that demons come from." He smiled and took a torch off the side of the wall and started down another cavern, letting the fire light his way.

She followed him, pausing with him as they came to a ragged curtain covering an entrance. "There are others here."

"Others like myself." He nodded and walked in, looking around the room. Each person, creature, busy with their own tasks. "Seraph." Leon snapped.

Seraph looked up in the corner from the wood carving in his lap. "What is it now? What puny wish have you promised we'd grant?"

Leon swept Cora into the firelight, her skirts swirled and her magic flared by instinct, demanding attention. Seraph stood, his body bent forward a little more than Leon, his hands just as lengthy and bony. It amazed Cora that this creature could hold a woodcarving tool at all.

"The Gypsy Lady." Seraph bowed, "it is a pleasure to grant your wish."

She bowed her head. "I need a new violin. Mine was destroyed by the Demon King."

"I can't believe he actually managed to catch you."

Seraph shook his head and went back to the stool he perched on. "I can grant you your wish. I will have it for you in two night's time. Will that work?"

A calm feeling swept over her and she welcomed the thought of holding a new violin. "That would be fine, thank you."

"I shall deliver it for you." He picked up a fresh block of wood and started to examine it. "You have a good evening."

She bowed her head and turned to leave with Leon. As he led her to the boat, she felt she had made a deal with the demons themselves, but with only the demand of ending the war, by a decree of fate, she refused to question the terms.

Leon took her back to the dock in the village, dropping her off in silence. She walked along the banks of the river, going over the events in her mind, when she saw the red eyes of her temperamental demon. Chuckling she held her arms out. "Come to take me back to your king?"

Darius stepped out of the shadows. "How can you be so stupid about this? You know he wants you back."

"Simply because I am a Demon Hunter now, and he, like my father, thinks I could be of use to him." She crossed her arms. "What are you doing here?" She resisted the urge to run to him and pull him close.

"My father wanted me here to watch the movement of hunters. Since the village to the north is almost to our borders, we're preparing to attack."

"You support his battle. Your father has been ruling in our world for way too long, why shouldn't we take it back?"

"I'm not saying that I agree to the principles behind it, nor the actions that has lead to this, but I can't fight him right now." He ran a hand through his hair, and her heart skipped a beat. "I am not strong enough."

She blinked a few times as the vision of him

killing his father flashed through her mind, erasing all thoughts of intimacy. "No, that's not right. You are, but not alone." She glanced to the north. "We need to postpone the battle. How long until the village to the north breaches the border?"

"Less than a week, they want to attack before the next full moon." He watched her. "Are you alright?"

She nodded. "Yes, how do you know their plans?"

"We have inside sources, too."

"Of course you do. I need to see if I can get my father to postpone his plans, and then you and I need to work on getting rid of your father." She turned away from him, taking a few steps as she thought. "Your father, he was fond of my mother, true?"

He nodded. "Yes, he speaks of her fondly still, even more fondly than my mother." Bitterness tinted his voice.

She turned back to him. "I'm going to use that to my advantage." She gave into her urges and kissed him. "You're going to have to trust me."

"Trust a witch?" He asked with a smirk. "I don't know about that."

She smiled at the term that he used. "And I don't know about trusting a demon, but I'll take my chances in this." She cursed as she heard the footsteps of boots against the cobblestone above them. "That's Alaster."

"I don't like the way he looks at you." Darius growled, turning his eyes to the road.

Cora laughed. "Getting a little overprotective are we? I don't belong to you."

He pulled her close, kissing her softly at first and then forcing his tongue between her lips. "The Gypsy Lady belongs to no one. Go take care of your suitor, I'll return to you when it is safe and we don't have an audience." He melted into the shadows, just as Alaster started to make his way down to the bank.

"Cora, something has happened." He took her hand. "Theresa is missing. The king is worried that she might have tried to come to the village, but none of the warriors can find her."

Fear rushed through her and she ripped her hand away from him to start climbing her way back up to the street, as the visions flashed in her mind. Her sister should have stayed with the other hunters, not left them and not disappeared. Worry replaced the fear, wondering if the king already killed Theresa or what he planned on doing with her in the meantime. She cursed as she slipped and stumbled a few steps up the hill. When she reached the street she found herself running back to her house.

"Cora wait." Alaster climbed after her and followed her down the street. "Your father wants you to lay low, he doesn't want you to get wrapped up in it."

She glared back at him. "I don't care what he wants. I need weapons, a cross bow, a knife, a sword." She saw the look he gave her. "Now, Alaster. I'm not playing damsel in distress here. I want weapons before sun up."

"And if I can't get them for you?" He tried to make it a threat.

She gave a wicked laugh. "Then I go in there with just my magic and rescue my sister that way."

"I can't let you do either, you know that." Alaster shook his head. "You aren't trained at all."

"I don't need the training." She snapped. "I was left alone in the village without any protection any training, or weapons and I survived just fine. I will not let my sister become victim to the Demon King." Cora turned away from him heading towards her home.

Alaster grabbed her hand and spun her to face him. "How do you know that she is with him? What makes you so certain?"

"Simple. I saw him kill her in a vision, remember? That is the only place that she would be, she is not as sly as I am and wasn't able to make it to the village without being followed." She ripped her hand away from him. "You have no idea how much she means to me, she is the only family that I still have left."

"Not true-"

"Don't you dare say that I still have my father, because that man means nothing to me, and I to him. I am nothing but a pawn for him in this war, and I will not let him or the Demon King use me."

Alaster's jaw tightened. "And what about the prince? Are you about to let him use you?"

"I'm sorry?" She narrowed her eyes at him. "What are you talking about?"

"We have people on our side of things too, that know exactly what happened between you and the prince." She couldn't stop the blush from gracing her cheeks. He scowled. "So it is true, he had his way with you."

She chuckled, "Yes, he had his way with me, and I with him. That is none of your concern."

"You know there is a chance that he got you pregnant." He hissed. "That you have contaminated the bloodline."

The thought had never crossed her mind. She rubbed her eyes. "Forget the bloodline." She threw her hands up in the air, frustrated with him. "It's nothing but trouble. I'm not going to sit here and argue with you, I have other things that need to be done."

"Right, we'll worry about the Demon Prince later. I'll get you your weapons, but you aren't going in there without me." He pushed passed her.

Cora entered her home and pulled her clock and mask off with a sigh. Hanging them by the fire she went through her plans in her mind, praying to whatever deity would listen she would be able to pull it off.

CHAPTER NINE

Theresa looked up at the bars of her cell in defeat. Watching the guard pace the dungeon. Nothing on her would allow her to even attempt to get a message to Cora. Fear started to settle in the pit of Theresa's stomach as she realized help would not be coming.

"The king would like to see you now." The guard pulled a set of keys from a pocket and unlocked the gate in front of her.

"I just bet he would." She stood and straightened out her skirt.

The guard grabbed her by her upper arm and yanked her out of the cell. "Glad to see that you think this is some type of joke."

"What's the worst that's going to happen? He's going to kill me?" She asked, trying to keep the fear out of her voice.

He shrugged. "If you aren't useful to him, yes. We've seen it before." He dragged her up stone stairs to the foyer, throwing her to her knees in front of the king.

Xavier narrowed his eyes. "This isn't Cora."

Theresa blinked, surprised at the comment. "Your

guards mistook me for Cora?" She tried to stop the laughter bubbling up in her throat. "She has red hair, I have brown, she's a bit taller than I am, and runs around in a corset most of the time."

"This is not funny." He said, anger bubbling below the surface. "She was the one I needed, not you. You're hardly any use to me." He snarled, his hand resting on the sword at his side. "Damn useless seer."

She scoffed. "I'm hardly useless to you. I've already helped you out tremendously when it came to the movement of the northern village."

"That is true." His hand inched away from the hilt. "Take her down to the seers, make sure she stays there. I want her with the talented ones, keep her shackled." He snapped, motioning to the guards. "If anything Cora will know that I have you and will come for you."

Cora tapped her booted toe against the ground, waiting for Alaster. Clad in men's pants and a loose blouse, she bounced back and forth between her feet, eagerness touched with panic crawling through her as the sun kissed the horizon. She pushed off the wall of the house and started to walk towards the woods, doubting his loyalty to her.

Frantic footsteps behind her made her pause and the sound of his voice stopped her completely. "Aren't you forgetting something?"

She spun around and smiled, his own weapons strapped to his back and hips and carrying a sling with her weapons. She examined the crossbow and then slung it across her back. "Excellent. How did you manage to get them so fast?"

He handed her a set of throwing knives and watched her strap them to her thighs. "I stole them from the armory."

She finished strapping them on and then reached for her sword. "I'm proud of you. I never thought that you would go against my father's orders."

"He doesn't even know I was there. It was unguarded when I went in." He shrugged.

Cora paused. "The armory is never unguarded."

"Strange I know, but we don't have the time to worry about that. Let's go." He started towards the village. "Do you know which realm they are keeping her in?"

"If she's a prisoner, she'll be in the human realm, because humans, witches or not, can't survive in the demon dungeon."

"Why?"

"I didn't ask, he didn't say."

"I have another question for you." He paused as they reached the outskirts of the village. "Why did you sleep with him?"

"I'm not talking about that with you. You aren't my father, you aren't my mate, and certainly it's not any of your concern. It was my choice." She shook her head and marched right passed him.

Alaster paused and she imagined he counted to ten before following her. "I'm simply concerned for your well being."

"Well, let me tell you, my well being is still very much intact after sleeping with Darius"

"So you're on a first name basis with him?" Alaster growled. "How is that for an enemy relationship, first he kidnaps you and then you fuck him, and now you're best friends."

"I don't see what your issue is with this." Dread started to fill her, only one reason came to her mind when she pondered why he cared so much.

"Your father promised me your hand in marriage once the Demon King was dead." He snapped. "So everything you do is my concern."

Cora froze, her hands curled into fists. "You've got to be kidding me."

Alaster went to her side and tried to take one of her hands. "No, he wants you with someone that can protect you and that can teach you. He doesn't know how the bonds are affecting your magic, so he's worried that your powers may disappear just as easily as they came."

"I don't care what he thinks and I certainly don't agree with this arranged marriage." She moved away from his touch and started further into the forest. Alaster went silent as she marched on, following behind her.

After a while he spoke up.

"It's at least a day's trek to the castle. Can't you summon a door?"

"I could, but we don't know who or what will be waiting on the other side." She traced her fingers over the hilt of her sword. "Then again, we would have the advantage of a surprise and be deep within the castle."

Alaster nodded. "I think it would be best. So draw us a door, my dear, so we can get this over with."

This could be her chance to help Darius kill his father. Her eyes scanned the woods before she stepped up to an oak. She couldn't help but wonder if Darius kept watch over her even now, if he overheard about her new betrothed. She put her hand up to the oak and muttered her words. The light appeared and she walked through, hand on the hilt of her sword and Alaster followed.

Alaster looked around. "Where in the castle are we?"

"Just outside the dungeon. We're going to see if Theresa is here, and then you're going to take her home." She turned to her left and headed towards the dungeon.

"I'm not leaving you here."

"You have no choice, this is our best chance to kill the Demon King, and I don't need Theresa around and in danger. You have to take her home." She tried to make her voice commanding.

A deep laugh made them both turn around. "I

don't think Theresa is going home, she's currently too busy serving as one of my seers."

Cora crossed her arms, not willing to draw a weapon yet, even though Alaster instantly drew his sword. "All I want is my sister back."

"And a chance to kill me. Does my son know that's your desire? I think it would break his heart to hear that you want to kill his father." Xavier laughed and looked at Alaster. "Put the sword away you have no chances against me. Both of you are weak as far as Demon Hunters are concerned."

"Alaster, listen to him, we're outnumbered." She said, putting a hand on his wrist.

Alaster shoved her away and rushed the Demon King. Xavier sidestepped the attacked and grabbed Alaster by the throat, throwing him down the hall. "Should have listened to the little magic user. She knows what she's talking about."

Guards surrounded Alaster, stripping him of his weapons and keeping him pressed against the wall. Cora glanced at him briefly and then turned her eyes back to Xavier. "All I want is Theresa back and safe."

"And all I want is for you to work with me." He said, smiling. Cora studied him; his teeth seemed to be more pointed and snarled than Darius, and then his face started to mold and melt as the rest of his body started to change.

"Run, Cora." Alaster screamed struggled against the guards. "He's changing. He'll kill you!"

Cora stumbled back, not realizing the sight of his change stunned her. She pulled out her sword and waited for him to attack. His large size would limit him in the hall; she would have the advantage.

Her sword clattered to the ground as Xavier slammed her into the wall, his clawed hands pined her to the wall, cutting into her skin and she felt the blood begin trickling down her arms. Alaster's screams echoed in her head as the room spun. She refused to be kept down by the blow. She brought her legs up and tried to kick Xavier away, but the black body of the beast didn't budge. The torch next to her flickered with her anger and panic, and she smirked. She fed her magic to the flame and watched it dance across the eyes of the beast holding her. He tossed her away, his voice full of pain as he wiped furiously at his face and the burns.

"Clever little bitch."

Cora landed in a heap, her breath catching. Luckily her idea had worked. She pulled herself up from the ground, her body aching from the collision. Alaster disappeared from her view, but she couldn't be bothered with that. She needed to focus. Her eyes found the torches on the walls and quickly counted them. Five. Five she could work with. She found her footing and held her hands up, concentrating on the beast moving towards her.

He hesitated now that he knew she could control fire. "Come Cora, if you fight me you know I can kill your sister. Just a word from me and the guards would stab her through the heart." A sinister grin crossed his face.

She paused, the flames hesitating with her. "Let Theresa go and we'll talk about what you want from me."

"She's happier where she is, why do you think she came back to me? Why do you think she let me catch her? She is more useful here. Your people frown upon those who can only foresee and can't use magic." He took another step forward, his claws on his feet tapping against the stone. "Let her be happy here."

Cora shook her head. "I want to see her. I want her out of here and I want her safe."

"And what are you willing to give?" He asked a wicked smile on his muzzle like face.

A foolish answer almost escaped her lips, when Xavier's eyes slid to a figure behind her. She started to turn just as the guard's hilt met with the back of her head, darkness spreading over her vision as she fell to the ground.

Darius paced the riverbed, waiting to see Cora doing her rounds. With the other magic users around, Darius refused to risk finding her during the day. He turned when he heard footsteps, not his Cora's though. No these were heavier. A soldier or a warrior.

"She's not returning." Alaster snapped at the demon, his crossbow out and pointed at Darius' heart. "Your father has probably killed her by now."

Darius raised a brow at the crossbow. "She is too important to him to kill. I've learned that, but what do you mean she will not be returning, how did my father find her?"

"Other than you leading him right to us? Telling him that we had plans to enter the castle tonight?" Alaster's hands shook. "She was to be my wife."

Darius' heart skipped a beat. "You went into the castle?" He snarled, "you let her go into the castle unprepared and you came back without her?" His hands formed fists at his side as he tried not to attack the Demon Hunter.

"You didn't know?" Alaster lowed the crossbow. "I thought it was you that had put the idea into her head. She wanted to rescue Theresa. The guards let me go, wanting me to get a message to Lucas. Since my Demon Hunter mark is on my chest and not visible to them, they spared my life."

Darius took in the information and cursed. "He has them both." He ran a hand through his hair, pacing. "I can't believe this."

Alaster shook his head. "You had nothing to do with this? I saw you with her last night, I saw you outside her home waiting for her last night."

"I was watching for her. I was worried that my father would send guards after her." He grumbled. "I didn't think she was stupid enough to waltz right into the castle."

Alaster laughed. "Her sister means the world to her, I think she'd have gone to hell and back if she could for Theresa."

"Yeah, so I've noticed. I'll see what I can do." Darius eyed the crossbow. "You watch where you point that thing. A guard would have killed you instantly for even having it out." He disappeared into the shadows, hoping he wouldn't be too late to get to Cora.

"Sir, if I may speak to you." Alaster's voice entered the library, disturbing Lucas and his men from looking over the map.

"What is it?" Lucas asked, not even looking up from the map.

Alaster took a deep breath. "Cora believes that Theresa was taken by the Demon King, and has run off to try and rescue her sister."

"She what?" Lucas' head snapped up and his eyes narrowed at Alaster. "You were supposed to bring Cora back here. You're telling me that she went after the king herself?"

Alaster gave a weak nod. "And she hasn't returned."

"It's nearly dusk, she probably has yet to make it to the castle." He muttered.

"Actually sir, I believe she used a door."

"She is not-" Lucas paused. "She is strong enough?" He asked, defeated.

"Yes sir, she used a door to get back here when I was first sent to the castle." Alaster murmured.

Lucas paced and looked at the map, thinking of how he could use this to his advantage. "We do not have much of a choice, we've lost two of our best cards. The village to the north has been slowed down by a land slide, and now I am sure the king would be expecting us to attack or try to bargain with him again."

"What about the girls though? Shouldn't they be

our first priority?" Alaster stepped up to the table. "Cora is the strongest of the Demon Hunter blood that has appeared in a long time, and Theresa is your true daughter, and a powerful seer. We shouldn't leave them in there."

"This is war, they were captured, the only way to get them back will be to storm the castle. We have to play our cards right. There must be a reason that Demon King wants them. I am betting that they are worth more to him alive than dead." The thought of his daughter in the demon's hell filled him with guilt, but he knew Theresa would be able to handle it.

"Yes; however, there are worse things than death." Alaster shook his head. "But you are leading this, I will follow your lead."

Theresa tugged on the chains attacked to her wrist that forced her to sit on a pillow in front of the pool. Nothing came to her since she arrived, her nerves too frazzled to even call on unwanted visions. She looked up when the door at the top of the stairs opened and the king walked in.

His hand clenched around something, and wicked smile crossed his face. "Hello, Theresa."

She bowed her head, "Sire."

"I see you remember your manners. I have some bad news for you, little one." He moved so that she could see him better. "Cora was killed."

Her body tensed, her fist clenched in her crossed legs, her breathing stopped for a moment and she moved her eyes to his. "What do you mean, killed?" Disbelief filled her, followed by anger causing her body to shake.

He opened his hand and showed her the lock of red hair. "She attacked me when she came looking for you. Damn shame, she could have been a good warrior and a powerful Demon Hunter, but she chose the wrong demon to attack."

"You lie." She raised her hand to touch the lock of Cora's hair. "You could have gotten this from her when you held her captive before." She moved it to see the blood coating his hands. Giving a slim smile she touched the blood, closing her eyes and forcing herself to see what happened. She saw the fight, how proud Cora seemed when she learned she could play with fire. She saw the guard behind Cora, ready to strike, and then the vision went black, a pain filling her head.

The king pulled away from her, "See, I speak the truth. Your sister is dead and you are now my personal seer. I assume you understand what that means?"

"It would be death to lie to you, and it is only you that I shall see for." She whispered, tears pooling in her eyes. "I have not seen anything since I have arrived here my lord, and it will take my mind a few days to recover from grief."

He nodded. "Very well, take your time. I have no need of you yet. I know that the northern village have been slowed down, and I know your father is hesitant in attacking because I have you."

"Does he know about Cora?" She closed her eyes, trying to imagine if her father would care or not about her sister's death.

He shrugged. "I sent her body back to the village." He stood. "I will come visit again in a couple nights. The guards will show you to your new chambers, where you will be kept for the days that you are not reading." He started back up the stairs, pausing for a moment, his back still turned away from her. "And Theresa, the moment you see something. I want to know, no matter how trivial you may think it is."

"Of course." She whispered, gazing into the water, seeing only images of Cora. "Of course." When the door shut behind him Theresa hunched over as the sobs took her over. Grief made her heart ache at the thought of her sister's death. The idea of never seeing her again made the tears come harder and the pain spread through her.

Cora awoke with a groan. Her body hurt, her head pounding, and a snarling noise filled her ears. She blinked a few times trying to get her eyes to adjust to the dark; after a couple minutes she could make out shadows. Bars, darker than those in the human realm, kept her trapped in the freezing cell of stone. The shackles on her wrist weighed more than what had been there before and with wider bands. She tried to call on magic to conjure a fire to see, but she could feel nothing. Absolutely nothing, not even a spark. She choked on panic as she continued to try and summon her magic, with no luck. A creature padded into view, his red eyes checking on the prisoner in the cell. The drool dripped off his snout, curling the fur there, and he bore his teeth at her with a warning.

Cora swallowed as she studied the hellhound, knowing exactly where she was. "I'm going to die." She whispered and scooted back until she hit the stonewall. "Please, please be dreaming."

"Not a dream, Gypsy Lady." A familiar voice came from her left. Leon looked at her, his own wrists in shackles. "The king has wanted you for many years."

"Why are you here?" She pulled her knees up to her chest, wrapping her arms around them the best she could.

Leon smiled at her. "Because the king wanted me to bring you to him, many pounds of gold he offered me. When he learned that I took you below the city for a new violin, he brought me here, afraid that I would provide you with something other than the thing you sought most."

"You shouldn't have to be here." She whispered. "Neither of us should be here, we did nothing wrong."

He laughed and it sounded cruel. "Nothing wrong? We have gone against the Demon King's wishes. You taught him that you could play with fire, that fire bent to your will, not the other way around. You proved to him that you are a worthy adversary, Gypsy Lady."

A squeak of a rusty door caused the hound to trot off and examine something.

"Go away, you pesky flea bag." A voice shooed the hound.

Cora's heart jumped. "Darius?" She ignored the look from the ferryman. "Darius?" She called again, trying to see through the darkness.

His face appeared near the bars. "Cora, you're alright."

"Relative term, get me out of here. Now." She begged. "And Leon, he has duties to return to."

Leon tilted his head to the side. "And what would the Gypsy Lady give to the prince for my freedom?"

"Leon has done nothing. He commissioned a violin for me, that is all. Please Darius?" She moved towards the bars.

Darius looked at the ferryman and then back to Cora. "You two know each other? Leon is one of the oldest water demons in existence, how on earth does he know you?"

"He used to ferry me down the river every night to meet clients. He took me below the city for a new violin." She whispered and looked at the boatman. "I never realized that you were demon."

He bowed his head. "Because you never looked for it, always a kind Gypsy Lady you were; you and your mother both. It is just sad that my time is up for serving you."

Cora turned to Darius, dreading the answer she asked. "What does he mean?"

"He is sentenced to execution, and there is nothing I can do to change that." Darius gave her sad eyes and reached a hand through the bars for her. "Leon has come to peace with it though."

Leon bobbed his head. "I have lived for many years and seen many things. I just wish I could live to see the end of this war."

"This isn't fair, he's in here because of me." Cora growled, trying to motion to Leon and then whimpered as her body protested. "Damn, I still hurt."

Darius appeared on their side of the bars. "You've only been out for a night and a day, your body hasn't healed. The shackles have to stay on, but my father is releasing you into my custody."

"Kinky." She snorted and held her arms up. "Your father wants me powerless, he fears me."

Darius laughed. "Of course he does! I saw what you did to his face. You're dangerous when you're cornered." He waved a hand and the chains fell from the shackles. "Your fiancé wanted you returned to him, but I wasn't able to arrange that."

Cora made a noise of disgust. "Not surprising. I'm not going back to him, even if I get out of here." She slowly stood, trying to make sure that everything worked. She looked back at Leon, her eyes sad. "I'm sorry, I will never forget what you did for me."

"Of course Gypsy Lady, and remember our deal." He bowed his head.

She smiled. "Of course," she turned and took the last few steps to Darius. "Thank you for coming."

He wrapped an arm around her and transported them to his room, giving her a second to gather herself before letting go of her. "I couldn't leave you in there. The hellhounds would probably make a snack out of you, and if not, then their master would have driven you mad."

She nodded and regretted it when pain hit her. "I can't feel my magic." She whispered, running her hands up and down her arms.

"Because of the shackles." He brushed his fingers over them, getting her to stop moving her hands.

She shivered. "I don't like it. I miss it already. I can't live like this."

"You won't have to for long. I'll get them off, but

we have to wait until my father is distracted and isn't likely to check on you randomly." He brushed her cheek. "I can't believe that I've missed you." He laughed slightly. "And the thought of that other...man touching you." He shook his head.

Cora laughed. "He never touched me, I never wanted him in that way." She placed a hand on his cheek. "This isn't going to work unless we get rid of your father, and you know that. The moment that he finds out we've been together he'll kill us." His skin felt warm against her hand, and she tried to stop the visions from creeping into her mind.

"Why? He sleeps with females all the time." He frowned. "What puts that haunted look in your eyes, Cora?"

Cora took a deep breath. "I was enlightened on a couple things while I returned home. Did you know that most Demon Hunters come from a pairing of demon and witch?" She watched as he shook his head. "Your father did, that's why he slept with my mother, and he was hoping my mother was the one with the power he sought. Turns out it wasn't, which is why he killed her when he found out that she slept with a Demon hunter and bore him a child."

"Which is you, the ferryman said something about keeping that secret from my father for the longest time, but when my father saw you-"

"He knew right away that I was Aura's daughter and the Gypsy Lady." She shook her head. "I don't know what he wants with my powers, but he's been looking for them."

"Fire, you can control fire." He thought for a moment.

Cora nodded. "Not only can I control it, but I can also conjure it."

"He could use you to destroy villages in an instant." His eyes widened. "I remember listening to him talk about a great fire that would threaten the villages and he would use that as his leverage to take them over." He looked at her, "But that was years ago."

She laughed. "He was searching for the starter of that great fire, wasn't he? Sending his guards into the village every night?"

"How did you know?"

"Because I was confined to my room during those raids, never allowed out without something hiding my features. I think my father knew the whole time." She sat on the bed, her body shaking. "Both sides only want me as a weapon."

Darius sighed and sat next to her. "Don't worry, we know how to end the war."

"Kill your father."

CHAPTER TEN

Xavier paced the room with the pools. "Have the Demon Hunters moved?"

"No sire, they sit and wait for the northern village." Theresa whispered. "The leader does not care that you have me, so he makes no move to save me." She looked into the pool, seeing visions of her father leaning over a table. "It is just a matter of time before the northern village gets the landslide cleared or find a way around it."

"Matter of time? Can you tell when they will arrive in the village?" He stopped behind her.

Theresa dipped her hand in the water watching the images change. "The night of the blood red moon, a fire will rage...somewhere."

"Where?" He snapped.

She shook her head. "It is unclear sire, but that is the night that the northern village will march on our village. Their numbers are great and their magic users skilled. They will meet with the group of Demon Hunters, and then they will march on the castle." She tilted her head to the side. "There, that is where the great fire is."

"Interesting." He grinned, and patted her head. "Do you see anything else?"

Theresa shook her head, "But I hear something. A child crying in the distance."

"Nonsense." He laughed. "Maybe they are crying because we will be victorious against the village. With the great fire on our side."

She bowed her head, not correcting him on his interpretation of the vision.

"I must say that you are one of the best spoils of war that I have gotten." He laughed and started towards the stairs.

Theresa smiled under her veil. Of course he would think that, he always heard what he wanted to hear from her. "Thank you, sire."

They spent the night with each other, Darius making it clear the he planned to claim his Gypsy Lady as fate intended. Still worn out from the night before he didn't register when Cora stirred. He tried to cuddle her closer as she moved around in the bed.

"Darius." Cora nudged his arms off of her as she climbed out of the bed.

"What?" He grumbled and then saw her go towards the window, watching her graceful movements. There on the bench under the glass sat a new violin made of dark wood.

The look of pleasure on her face made him smile. She drew the bow across the string and let out a peaceful sigh. "He did a great job on it. Look at this craftsmanship." She grinned, holding it up for him to examine. "Seraph did a great job on it."

"It looks just like the one you had before." He stood from the bed and took it from her and examining it. "It's beautiful." He held it out for her. "Play for me?"

She took it back from him and started playing an upbeat tune, her feet dancing to the notes in the faint moonlight. Darius sat back on the bed and watched as the happiness flowed through her as she swayed and danced across the room. He loved the way she glowed as she played; not a note faltered, nothing led her astray as she moved. Darius snarled as the notes went silent and guards grabbed him from behind shoving him to his knees.

"What is the meaning of this?"

One of the guards yanked his head up. "The king would like to see you and your whore."

Cora set the violin down on the bench avoiding Darius' gaze. Anger coursed through him at the insult the guards flung at his witch and he tried to pull out of the guard's grip while being pulled up. Both he and Cora remained silent as the guards forced them through the halls and up the tower where his father waited.

"A little rough to have your own son forced up here by guards, is it not?" Darius snapped, pulling his arm away from the guard's now loose hand.

Xavier turned from the window and met his son's gaze. "The girl will be staying with me."

Cora paled. "What, why?"

Darius waited for the answer, trying to resist any urge to reach out to comfort Cora. He needed to trust her and keep up their charade.

"Because I cannot risk him reproducing with you." Xavier walked towards her and grabbed her chin. "I know you have been sleeping with him."

Darius opened his mouth, but Cora laughed. "Jealous? That he could bed me without force, which you couldn't do with my mother?"

The sound of flesh against flesh echoed through the room and it took Cora a moment to recover from the backhand. Xavier looked at his son. "You have disappointed me. You could never rule as king. You are weakened by human flesh."

Darius shook his head, trying to keep his anger

down. "I don't see her responsible for the sins of the past, she is innocent of all the claims that you have against witches."

"Magic users are what brought us down before, it is only through dominating them that we have risen above them." Xavier yanked Cora away from the guard, and pull out a knife. Laughing he put the blade to Cora's pale neck. A guard grabbed Darius' arm when he made a move forward, preventing him from getting to his father.

Xavier gave a wicked laugh. "We used to slaughter them, burn their villages, kill them all, women and children. Then we learned that we could control them." He put a little bit of pressure on the blade. "That we could use them to our advantage and keep them weak. That was until someone slept with one, thinking that the pleasure of the body was worth the risk."

Darius watched as Cora closed her eyes and held herself still. He reminded himself that she could react appropriately under pressure. "And that was where the first Gypsy Lady came from, the first Demon Hunter."

"Exactly, we don't want more of those around. It ends with her." He laughed when panic caused Darius to jerk in the guard's grip. "Don't worry, I won't kill her yet. I need her to help me fight off the village to the north with her fire."

Darius swallowed. "Are you so sure it will work?"

"My seer told me such, she proclaims that it is how we will protect the castle from them." He gave a manic laugh and tossed Cora to a guard, away from Darius. "And you son, will be staying in the demon realm and away from her."

Darius took comfort from Cora's steady gaze and tiny nod of assurance. "As you wish."

Xavier smiled. "Take her to my rooms in the human realm, and do not let her go near the seer pools."

A strange look crossed over Cora's face and Darius raised a brow when she smirked. "I'll see you later lover." She winked at him and went with the guards without a fight.

Darius snorted and inclined his head as she passed by. She asked him to trust her, so he would have to, and hope she pulled through.

Cora looked around the room the guards left her in. It reminded her much of the one at her father's place with a mattress on the floor and a fur blanket to cover up with. She rolled her eyes and went to the window to look out on the forest. She needed to find a way to escape the room, find Theresa and get away. Rummaging through the drawers she discarded the useless items until she spied a tray sitting at the foot of the bed. She shifted through the items there and happened upon a dinner knife. Happily, she rushed to the door and went to work picking the lock.

After a few minutes she heard the satisfying click of the tumbler. Opening the door, she looked down the hall and didn't spot any guards. With a sigh of relief she walked out of the room, wishing she had her weapons with her as she heard noises down a nearby hall. She crouched and crept against the wall, looking for shadows and praying the guards would not chose this route.

"The king would like his seer brought to him."

"Did he say why? Normally he goes to see her."

"He apparently has something important to ask her, and he does not want her at the pools. He also wants to make sure that there is an archer there."

"He suspects that she is lying?"

"Yes."

Cora paused, waiting for her moment to follow them to Theresa. With a deep breath she followed the voices and the footsteps, stopping when she saw their backs. They removed a bar from the giant wooden door. She swallowed, trying to decide how to take the two out without a weapon. When the door opened it revealed a steep staircase leading down and she saw her chance. Pushing away from her hiding spot, she rushed the two, knocking them off their feet and down the stairs.

The bodies landed at the bottom with a thump, blood pooled around the heads and she heard the gasp of someone below. "Theresa?"

"Cora? What are you doing here? I thought, I thought you were dead." Theresa pulled against the chains trying to get off her pillow. "You have to leave, he wants you dead."

"No he wants me for my power." Cora carefully made her way down the stairs and over the bodies. "What happened, how did he get you?" She looked at the chains holding her sister in place and sighed. "I have no magic."

"The guards, they should have the keys."

Cora searched the bodies and found the keys to her sister's shackles. She went and got the chains off. "He knows that you are the true Gypsy Lady now, the fire starter."

"Yeah because I swiped fire across his face as he was trying to have me contained. Don't worry about me, we need to get you out of here and safe."

"And what about you?"

"Darius and I are going to kill the king and stop the war."

"You make it sound so easy." Theresa rubbed her wrists. "But there are bound to be more guards." She paused as a shadow appeared at the top of the stairs.

Cora took a deep breath as Xavier snarled down at them. "How did you manage to get out of the room?"

"You know, I've had to live without magic before. It's called a survival skill."

He shook his head, "Does not matter, I know the outcome now, I know how the battle will end." Behind him came a guard with a bow and arrow. "Your sister was nice enough to share that you will protect the castle for me with your fire."

The news struck Cora and she whipped around to face Theresa. "What?"

"I told him that there was a big fire in the castle when it was stormed. He took it as he wanted, I don't know exactly what it means."

Xavier raised his hand and the archer aimed at Theresa. Cora put herself in front of her sister. "I will not let you kill her."

"You cannot stop it, she will die. She has outlived her usefulness. That is the way things are done here."

Cora shook her head. "No."

"Ask Darius. He will be dead soon enough, but I need him around to keep you working for me."

Another piece of surprising news, but Cora stood her ground, "Why don't you let me have my magic back and then we can find out who truly would win the battle."

"I cannot do that, I know that if given the chance you would kill me without question." Xavier laughed, and more guards pushed passed him. "Take the whore and leave the seer, she and I have some unfinished business."

Cora struggled as the guards grabbed her. "Let go of me."

He laughed, "You know what, let her stay, watch her sister die as we learn the truth about the war."

"I haven't seen the end of the war. I can't tell you how it ends."

"Then you better ask for guidance, because you need it."

"What does it matter, either way you'll kill me." Theresa gave an angry laugh.

Cora froze "Don't give in to him Theresa, he needs you to see the future for him. If you don't see anything then you haven't served your purpose."

"Your sister brings up a valuable point. It's time to change tactics. You don't tell me what you see and I will torture your sister. You will watch her blood flow as you pled and beg for guidance. Obviously neither of you fear death."

"Be strong sister of mine." Cora took a deep breath.

"I won't tell you anything, because I have seen nothing past the great fire." Theresa said, glancing at the archer. "I know you can tell if I'm speaking the truth. Not even the old crone has foreseen the future of the war."

He growled. "But you are supposed to be different." He looked at the guards holding Cora. "Chain her up at the end of the pool. Call on the guard of the hellhounds and make sure he knows that there is another victim up here for him."

"And what would you like him to do to her?" The guard asked as his companion dragged a struggling Cora to the end of the pool. They shoved her to her knees so she mirrored Theresa's normal position.

Xavier grabbed Theresa by the hair and dragged her back to her pillow, chaining her there. "Tell him what ever he would like, but don't kill her. I can't have her dead."

"I shall let him know." The guard bowed his head and disappeared up the stairs, stepping over the dead bodies.

Xavier stroked Theresa's hair. "Now you do not want to see your sister get tortured, do you?"

"I will be strong for her, just like she is for me." She whispered, not looking up at the guards stripping Cora of her clothes, preparing her for whatever the guard of the hellhounds would do.

Cora closed eyes her as new chains connected to the bands on her wrists, tethering her to the floor. Fear pulsed through her as she thought about how to warn Darius or how to free Theresa. A shiver ran over her as the air danced across her naked body. She looked up at Xavier with hate in her eyes as he pulled on Theresa's hair again. "You will pay for this."

"Tough words for someone that is going to be tortured. Your sister will learn her lesson, and you will be too weak to even think about attacking me." He laughed. "Then you will exhaust yourself trying to protect this castle from the north village."

She shook her head as the guards forced her face down to the edge of water, the pebbles biting into her skin. "You wish. Darius will find a way to bring you down, and you will lose this war. The time of the demons is over."

"And the magic users will rise? Really, what have they been teaching you out there? Your mother was just as blind as you are." He knelt next to Theresa, "you will have to tell me when you see things, or you will see your sister suffer."

"I am prepared for that." She whispered

"And are you prepared for her to lose the child that she carries?"

Both of the girls balked. Cora shook her head. "Don't listen to him, I'm not pregnant."

"Alaster was right? You slept with the demon?" Theresa asked, her voice appalled.

Cora tried not to roll her eyes. "Really, does that matter right now?" She thought for a moment and smirked, feeding her sister's anger. "Well if you must know, yes, I did sleep with him and it was wonderful."

"I'm not lying about the child, it happens when a demon sleeps with a Demon Hunter." Xavier looked down at Theresa.

"Except that's not the way it worked with my mother, or I would be your child." She laughed, "he is lying."

Xavier nodded. "It does not change the fact I can sense the life growing inside you, Theresa that child you heard crying in your vision I am betting it was Cora's. Could you see the mother?"

"No, I couldn't see the child, I could only hear it." Theresa whispered, her eyes narrowed at Cora. "You betrayed us. You slept with him."

Cora shook her head. "I betrayed no one. I have no loyalties."

"Not true, you have family." Theresa begged. "You need to think of them-"

"I have you and that is it." Cora said. "And soon I won't even have that. Let them torture me, do not give them anything."

"You deserve the pain that you will receive for thinking that you have nothing." She snapped, her eyes aglow with disgust.

The anger burning in Theresa would allow her to look past the pain of Cora's torture. Cora smiled at the king. "See, it doesn't matter what you do, she always has everyone's best interest at heart. So torture me, do your worst."

"And the child?" He muttered, walking towards her. "Is not all life precious to magic users?"

She nodded, "But there is no life inside me but the flame. If you recall, my magic was minimal at the time that we had sex, because of the bonds. The magic between your son and I is what caused the magic to grow, there was no conceiving of a child there. Nothing but pure passion between us." Of course she didn't see the need to mention the night before.

"And now he thinks of nothing but you and doing what you want him to." He growled. "You have ruined my perfect son." He kicked her, causing her to jerk in her chains. "I will make sure that the hellhound master has his way with you. He is a master at bending the mind to insanity."

"I can't wait to see his magic." Cora looked up at Theresa whose hair hid her face as she looked in the pool. "And you know, I doubt he's all that scary. I was in your demon hell and didn't even feel a lick of power there." Cora said, trying to distract the king from noticing Theresa having a vision. Her mind drifted to the ferryman and she wondered if he had faced his death yet. "Though I think I saw a ghost from the past, someone my mother once trusted dearly. Someone who danced with her when she got her first violin."

"Ah yes, Leon, the demon of the boat." He laughed. "He loved you very much, it is a shame I had to kill him for hiding you from me. I'm sure you will be seeing his ghost around much more often. The master of the hellhounds will use anything he can against you to bend your mind." He glanced back at Theresa. "Even her. And I am sure she will love seeing it all happen."

Theresa continued to look down her hair covering her face, oblivious to her surroundings. Cora took a deep breath. "We're sisters, no matter what we'll stand together." Her confidence faltered a little with her words.

"If you say so. Now if you would excuse me, I have to deal with my son. Enjoy your stay in the seer area." He kicked her again and then headed back up the stairs, stepping over the dead bodies.

Cora closed her eyes. "Theresa?"

"Don't talk to me. I'm beyond angry at you."

"Because I slept with him."

"Because you could be carrying his child." Theresa hissed. "What is wrong with you, why would you risk that with a demon?"

Cora gave a bitter laugh, "I was drunk, and we were both needy. We both saw it as a mistake after." For a little while, she added silently.

"You don't expect me to believe that do you? I've seen the way he looks at you Cora, I've seen the way he loves you and the way he will mourn when he holds your bleeding body." She snapped. "And the child-"

"I thought you didn't see the child." Cora swallowed, shifting to get as comfortable as she could on the floor and trying to sense if she had made a mistake about being pregnant.

"I didn't, I merely heard it. But that child needs a mother to guide her and love her." She whispered. "I can't teach her the way of the Gypsy Lady. You have to do that. You have to teach her to find that joy within the music, the violin."

Cora took a deep breath, her body starting to shiver with the cold air. "You went from being angry to already mourning my death. If you heard the child, that means there are at least nine months before that can happen. We have time to prevent it. Darius won't let me die." In that moment she realized the truth, Darius did hold her heart and she would do anything for the demon.

"I don't know if we can prevent it." Theresa's voice softened as she looked back down at the pool of water.

The door at the top of the stairs creaked open as a man dressed in black leather came down, the hellhound from the dungeon trotted behind him. Cora closed her eyes and prayed to anyone who would listen that she would survive.

Xavier walked into Darius' study and laughed. "Hello my son."

Darius straightening from the map on the table, "I thought you were done with me. You have what you want."

"Oh yes, the Gypsy Lady. She is proving to be very helpful to me." Xavier glided over and looked at the map. "I see you have the northern tribe marked out."

"What do you mean that she's been helpful? She's been locked in your room since you've taken her." Darius tried to hide the sick feeling sliding through him, but the suspicion in his eyes betrayed him.

Xavier laughed. "She managed to pick the lock to my door and sneak out. She was trying to find her sister. Killed two of my guards in the process. Now she is being used to persuade her sister to tell me what future she sees."

"You're having her tortured." Darius managed to keep his face blank this time. "The hellhound master, that's where he was going, to the seer pool."

"Why do you care? She is simply a magic user." Xavier looked at the map, "This plan will not work. We should just kill the village off before they hit our village."

Darius welcomed the change in topic, forcing thoughts of Cora away. "It would work, but then we have to worry about retaliation from our own village, because by the time we get to the northern warriors, they will be close to us. It would seem like a massacre to our village."

"Why would I worry about that, they all know what we are capable of. It would put even more fear into our people." Xavier shrugged. "That is the only way that you can rule humans, through fear and their emotions."

Darius shrugged. "I don't know about that, it isn't how the northern village seems to work. I know that's how demons are, but humans are much more...persuadable."

"You think so? Is that how you got your magic user pregnant?" Xavier asked, slamming a hand down on the map.

Darius froze. Closing his eyes, he tried to recall the night he spent with Cora, always touching her; she never left his arms. He didn't feel anything different about her and she didn't mention anything. "You're lying."

"Why would I lie about such?" Xavier turned to face his son. "You have created another Demon Hunter, unless I take care of the problem."

"I didn't feel another life form in her. She isn't carrying a child." The sick feeling came back, but he pushed it off.

"Then maybe it is not yours. Didn't you say that she had a lover with her father's people?"

"No, I said she had a betrothed, and I know she hasn't slept with him." Darius turned his back to his father. He needed to get to Cora to see if Xavier spoke the truth, perhaps the child hadn't formed yet when he last saw her, but that couldn't be right. Her absence from him should have been long enough for the child to be developed. He should have felt the child, even if she conceived the night before.

Xavier laughed. "I have you questioning her loyalty now. See humans and magic users alike use their emotions to get what they want. That is why we can use emotions to control them."

"She didn't use me, and she didn't sleep with him." He mumbled and crossed his arms. "Either way, I hadn't felt a child in her when she was with me, so you lie."

Xavier shrugged. "Believe what you will. Now, I need you to lead part of the army against the northern village."

"Of course you do, because that puts me out of your way. What are you planning?" Darius narrowed his eyes, his fist clenching at his side.

"Do not worry about it and listen to my orders."

"Of course." He spat before spinning on his feet and walked out.

Alaster stormed into the main room where Lucas stood in front of the fire. "The north villagers have been intercepted."

Lucas turned and frowned. "What do you mean intercepted?"

"The king's men have gotten to the pass where they were supposed to get past the landslide." Alaster swallowed. "And I have received news of your daughters."

"A messenger?"

"Yes."

"Why was I not informed of his arrival?"

"Because he greeted me in the village when I was watching over the house. He told me that Theresa had become the king's personal seer and that Cora was under the care of the Hell hound master." Alaster whispered. "Both are still alive, but I fear that may not last much longer."

Lucas nodded. "It may not last too much longer. They know Cora's bloodlines, and Theresa will not be able to hold up much longer. She truly is the weaker of the two."

"So what now?" Alaster moved closer. "We leave them there? We attack the castle on our own? Or do we aid the north villagers?"

"We need to aid the north villagers, but we can't put too many of our men out there. I'm sure that is what the king is waiting for." Lucas turned to the table behind him and looked over the map. "If only we knew the weaknesses of the castle and king's men."

"Simply cut off the snake's head and the rest dies." Alaster said gently. "Kill the king and the rest of the demons should crawl back into whatever little hole they came from."

"Just like when they came here. So now we need to know how to get to the king." Lucas tapped the picture of the castle on the map.

"I think I know how." Alaster said. "You're not going to like it, but I think it's the only chance that we have."

"Water." Cora whispered, "I need water."

Theresa's eyes flickered up and then back down. Guilt filled her as she watched her sister suffer, but anger still brewed under the surface adding to the feeling of being betrayed. "I cannot serve you and you know that. Do not beg, do not plead, because I will not risk my life for you right now."

Cora closed her eyes. "I need to see Darius."

At the name, the fury took over and Theresa growled, not understanding how her sister could count on the demon. "So that he can have his way with you again?" Theresa snapped and then went quiet as the door opened. Heavy footsteps descended the stairs, and stopped right by Theresa. Her heart skipped a few beats, waiting for him to ask his question.

"Have you seen anything?" The king's voice boomed through the room.

Theresa shook her head. "Nothing of substance, nothing you didn't already know, the rebels are moving to help the northern tribes."

"What of my son?" He grabbed her hair and pulled her head back. "Is he betraying me?"

Pain flooded through her scalp and her eyes flickered to her sister's shivering form. "No, he didn't mean to impregnate her. He thought of her simply as a whore."

Cora closed her eyes at the words. Theresa turned away when her sister started to dry heave and the hellhound trotted up. A scream echoed through the room as Cora tried to tear herself away from the chains.

With a deep breath Theresa confirmed the lie. "Really, Darius thinks of her only as a toy."

Xavier let go of her hair and moved towards the shaking girl at the other end of the pool. "Then mayhap I should give you back to my son. He does like to spoil his whores."

The girl didn't respond, locked in whatever nightmare the hellhound master gave her. Xavier nudged her with his foot and smiled. "Of course you wouldn't be much use to him now. Powerless, stripped and naked. He likes fight to his women."

The king spun away from her and started back up the steps. "Theresa, if I find you're lying to me, I will kill Cora. You will watch and it will haunt you for the rest of your life in my service." He slammed the door shut behind him, the lock clicking in place.

Theresa looked at her sister, trying not to imagine what she saw to cause the tears to stream down her cheeks and her body jerk in such pain.

Darius walked to the arch of the bridge, wondering why Alaster called him to meet. The full moon bathed the water in light and Darius thought about his Gypsy Lady, hoping she survived and wanting to hold her. Footsteps on the stone brought his attention back to in front of him.

Alaster stood there, no weapons, no cloak, hiding nothing from the demon. Darius thought the man either foolish or very brave. "Hello hunter, to what do I owe this pleasure? You took a great risk trying to contact me."

"I know that you want the king dead." Alaster crossed his arms. "I also know that for some reason of your own, you care for Cora."

Darius body stiffened at the mention of his Gypsy. "I'm listening."

"One of our intelligence teams told us that Cora is currently under the care of the hellhound master and that Theresa is a personal seer to the king." Alaster watched as Darius gave a nod confirming what had just been said. "And like I said, I know you want the king dead. We want to help you."

"What you're saying is that you want to be allies?" Darius raised a brow. "Trade information, for what? Cora's and Theresa's safety?"

"For your help on killing the king, that's all. We don't want you to promise anything else. However, I believe that you're going to need Cora's help with killing the king. She is a true Demon Hunter, she is the one that our myths speak of." Alaster sighed. "She wants you, she trusts you."

Pride filled Darius as he heard those words, but it faded when he spoke. "The Hellhound master is using that against her. I don't know if she'll be in any shape to fight if I can manage to rescue her from him." He paced the span of the bridge. "My father is using her to keep Theresa in line and giving true interpretations of the visions that she has been having."

Alaster bit his lip. "So Cora will be tortured until Theresa outlives her usefulness."

Darius knew the other man cared for the Gypsy and sighed. "Exactly. I've been forbidden to go back to the castle, so if I go in, I'm risking my life and the girls' lives. Unless you can find a way to get the king and most of his men out of the demon realm castle."

Alaster smirked. "What about an attack on the human realm castle?"

"That should draw him out, but you may lose many men." He shook his head. "I don't know if that's worth the risk to you right now."

"You have no idea what I'm capable of. You know how Cora can control fire as her magic?" He asked, flexing a hand.

Darius laughed. "Yes, she used it to blind my father during a fight. Apparently it was very impressive."

"Each Demon Hunter has something that they can control, mine is the dead. There have been plenty of people killed outside those gates, so I will have many people to work with to create an attack real enough that your father will have no choice but to come out."

"Impressive indeed." Darius bowed his head. "Make your attack and I will go rescue the girls. I will try to get Cora back to fighting shape, but I do not know how long it will take."

"If you must hide her somewhere, contact the boat men, there are those who are willing to hide they Gypsy Lady still."

"Of course." Darius bowed his head. "I wait for your attack."

CHAPTER ELEVEN

Darius took himself to the door of the seer pool, after throwing the bar away and yanking the door open he ran down the stairs, looking for Cora. He saw her at the far end of the pool, the Hellhound sniffing at her cheek. A shiver racked her body and he ran to her, at his approach the dog licked her and ran. With a great shuttering breath Cora's body heaved as she tried to pull away from him.

"Cora?" Darius asked, kneeling down next to her. He looked over at Theresa. "How long has she been like this?" He smoothed Cora's hair back, before going to Theresa and using magic to remove her chains.

Theresa stood and ran shaky hands over her dress, trying to straighten it. "It's been about a week since the hellhound master's first visit. She mumbles incoherently now and tries to scream. It's almost like she's constantly stuck in a nightmare."

"The Hell Hound uses it's masters power to inflict damages on the victims mind. Using anything they see or hear around them." He went back to Cora, he touched the chains and they fell away from her. With slow movements he picked her up, cradling her against him. "I need to get you to the boatmen, and safe. Cora is staying with me."

Theresa shook her head. "I'm not leaving her, even if she did betray us, she is my sister."

"She didn't betray you, she's not carrying my child, and it doesn't matter that we slept together. What is with you people?" He growled at Theresa. "You know the story of how the Gypsy Lady came to be. That's where the bloodline comes from." He held Cora close as her body thrashed in his arms and weakly attempted to push at his chest.

"Yes I know that, but times have changed." Theresa followed him up the stairs.

Darius paused and looked down the hall before exiting. "And they will change again, as soon as Cora is back up to fighting and the king is dead."

"Either way I'm not leaving her. You need me to take care of her. She's convinced that you wanted her as nothing more than a whore." Theresa looked down. "I had to tell your father something when I saw that you two were to be together again. Something to take suspicion away from you."

He groaned. "Fantastic, I can only imagine what nightmares came from that. We're known for being harsh to women, stupid legends. Fine, you can stick around, but do not leave the room that I'm putting you both in. Got it?"

"Like I have a wish to be chained back at that pool." She said with a soft laugh. "I need some clothes for her, food and water. Do you know how to get those binds off?"

Rumors spoke of the family of magic users who made the binds for criminals and the king took advantage of them when he conquered the kingdom. Darius knew who he must see and convince to help. "I'll have to call for someone who knows them, it could take me a day or two."

"If you trust them, fine, bring them. If not, do not worry about it, I'll find a way."

He shook his head. "It's not a matter of trust, it's a matter of sneaking him in here. Place your hand on my shoulder. I'm just going to take us to the rooms, don't want to risk the guards seeing us."

"How did you get in here in the first place? The king was supposed to have a guard keep you away from the castle." She took his hand without hesitation and closed her eyes against the transportation.

He looked around the nearly empty room he planned to keep the girls in. The bed was big enough for the two of them, a desk took up a corner, and there was a washroom off to one side. "Alaster faked an attack on the human castle, forcing my father and many of his guards to leave this one."

"He used his abilities?" Theresa asked, surprised.

Darius nodded. "Was he not supposed to?"

"No, it's just his is rare and a lot of Demon hunters are uncomfortable with him for it." She shrugged and watched him lay Cora on the bed.

Cora groaned and curled around herself, her eyes still shut. Darius went to reach out and touch her hair, but Theresa caught his wrist. "You go take care of finding the man to remove the bonds. Let me take care of her, please."

"Fine, I'll have a servant deliver the things you have requested." He turned his back on the girls, not wanting to think about the things Cora continued to see.

"Thank you. Hopefully I'll have her in a stable condition before you get back."

"Have you ever dealt with a hellhound victim before?" He asked, his voice a whisper in the room.

"I have." Theresa sighed. "Now go, please, I need those items."

He walked out the door and sighed. He grabbed the first servant who passed him and instructed her on what to do, before he flashed himself to the edge of the riverbank, where Alaster waited.

"She is safe?" Alaster asked, his hand gripping the hilt of his sword.

"They both are. Theresa insisted on staying with Cora to help with the damage done. She'll be an asset in Cora's recovery." Darius crossed his arms and sighed. "She needs to heal fast so we can kill the king, but I need someone to remove the bonds on her." He met eyes with Alaster.

"No."

"You know you are the only one who can remove those. Your family is the creators of those stupid things." He snapped. "I know you can remove them."

Alaster froze. "You know?"

"Yes, I know. I know all about you, since the first night that you left Cora in the village to when her father offered you her hand in marriage. Her father thought that you two would make a great couple, especially if Cora ended up coming into her magic. I saw you in the crowd the night that the king took her from the stage, I saw how much you wanted to fight to save her, but you just left her there." He narrowed his eyes. "You could have raised an army of the dead to save the woman that you love, but you didn't."

"You don't know what it's like, to be the outcast of your people. Cora was my chance to climb back to the top, and she is a strong woman, not weak like many of our kind."

"She's stronger than you'll ever know. Now you'll come with me and remove those bonds. Her magic will help her heal." Darius uncrossed his arms. "You've failed her before, do not let her pay for your mistakes."

Darius watched as Alaster looked up at the waning moon. A look crossed his face as if he imagined something. "And when the king is dead, and she is free? What then?"

"You let her make her own choice on where she

wants to go, and who she wants to be with." Darius shrugged. "At this point I doubt she has any ties that she wants to keep." The thought hit him hard. He wanted to hold on to her, but he knew the more he tried, the more she would want to be free.

"You don't like that idea any more than I do. Demon, I actually saw pain cross your eyes. You love her."

"Since the moment I first saw her." He glanced at the water.

Alaster shrugged. "Her heart has always been free, that's why she's the Gypsy Lady."

"Then let's free her again." Darius held his hand out. "I'll take you in, and I'll take you out. All you have to do is get those bonds off her."

After a moment of hesitation, Alaster took the offered hand.

Cora opened her eyes and groaned. The light from the fire seared her eyes and she tried to roll over, only to be held in place by a gentle hand. She took a deep breath and looked up at her sister. "Water." Pain weaved its way through her body with every little move she made.

Theresa gave a sigh of relief and went to get a mug of water. She helped her sister sit up and tipped the drink to her lips. "I'm surprised you're awake so soon."

Cora tried to gulp down the liquid, sputtering a little as she did. When she finished she laid back against her sister. "I ache, I'm sure these have something to do with it." She motioned to one of the bands on her wrist and mourned when her magic still didn't answer.

"Your magic helps you heal." Darius' soft voice came from the shadow. Alaster stood next to him, silent, arms crossed.

Cora closed her eyes against the visions that

lingered from the nightmares. "Not real, just dreams." She whispered and felt her sister's arms wrap around her in a comforting hug.

"That's right, neither of these men want to hurt you." She whispered against Cora's ear. "Both of them love you."

Cora gave a soft laugh. "You told me that Darius thought of me as a whore."

Darius stepped forward, ready to speak, but Alaster put his hand in front of the man. "Don't, let Theresa explain."

"I told the king that, because it was what he needed to hear and it will be to your advantage when he comes and finds you two in bed again." She stroked her sister's hair. "It will be what allows you to kill him."

She blushed at the mention of being in bed with Darius again. "And Alaster, what brings you to the demon realm?" She pulled the blanket up higher, not wanting him to gain a glimpse of her naked flesh.

"I came to remove your bonds." He said easily, "But now that I know what the plans are, I think I'll just deactivate them."

She blinked. "I'm sorry, what?"

"If you plan on seeing the king again, he'll notice if they have disappeared. I can deactivate the magic in them though, so that he thinks that you are still bound. It would play better into the whore perspective too." He tried not to spit the word out.

Cora's mouth opened, but she closed it and shook her head. Leaning back into her sister she tried to clear her thoughts.

Darius moved forward. "How are you feeling?"

"Better, I'm exhausted, but I'm sure that will fade with some rest." Cora gave him a weak smile. "Thank you, for coming for me."

Darius took her hand. "I couldn't leave you there, the thought of you under the hellhound master was killing me."

"So what now?" Theresa asked. "The king is bound to notice we're missing. I haven't seen anything relating to that."

"Alaster, you need to take Theresa home, her life is in danger if she stays here." Cora tried to sit up on her own, pulling away from her sister.

"You've seen something." Theresa slipped out from behind Cora and turned to look at her. "What did you see?"

Cora met her sister's eyes. "Your death." She whispered as a servant slipped into the room.

"Forgive me, my prince, but the king is calling for his seer, I thought it would be best that I come warn you."

Cora closed her eyes against the words, silently cursing.

Theresa bowed her head. "Tell him I escaped my captors and I will be right there." She stood from the bed and grabbed her veil and headed to the door.

"Don't Theresa, you won't survive."

Theresa glanced back at her sister. "It's my time, this will bide you time to heal. Darius can fake that he rescued us from Alaster, who came to save us after staging the attack." She pulled the veil over her face and walked out.

Cora stood and tried to follow her, only to stumble with the blankets wrapped around her. Darius caught her and pulled her close. "She is right." He whispered. "Let's get you taken care of and not let her sacrifice go to waste."

Her sister, the only family she truly loved walked out. Tears filled Cora's eyes, only to spill over and cause her to start sobbing. Darius wrapped his arms around her and kissed her head.

Theresa walked into the king's main room, her head bowed, "Forgive my tardiness my king."

Xavier looked up at an archer, who readied the

bow. "You were missing from the pool. What happened?" He snarled. "You did not warn me about the attack on the human castle, nor about a trespasser here."

Her face betrayed nothing as she knelt in front of him. "I did not foresee those events, my lord. Some things are not revealed to me. I have managed to escape my captor, though Cora is still with him."

"Do you know who it was?" He crossed his arms and leaned back in the chair.

She closed her eyes, thinking on the name and description. "His name is Alaster, from the Demon Hunters, he has hair as black as night, and his eyes are nearly white. He carries the power of death raising."

"He is a necromancer." He stroked his chin and stood. "And your sister, where is he keeping her?" Xavier watched as Theresa stayed still, but her eyes glanced to the archer who drew back on the bow.

"I have foreseen your son pulling her from Alaster. He missed his whore."

"Very well, I shall visit my son soon." The king raised and dropped his hand, several arrows hit their mark.

Theresa's body fell to the ground with a lifeless thump and Xavier looked over at the old crone who stood in the shadows. "Dispose of her body. She has served her purpose."

"And what of the other girl, the Demon Hunter that you seek?" The crone asked as she approached her dead student.

Xavier paused and looked towards the door, contemplating. "She still serves a purpose, even if no one can foresee it."

"She is too powerful of a creature to be bound by the laws of fate." The old woman said, looking down at the body.

Xavier shook his head. "Everyone is bound by the laws of fate. That is why your powers work, no one can allude them."

143

"The Gypsy Lady is different. She is an instrument of fate herself, and can weave through its laws. You should have known that when you met Aura and how she danced her way into your life and then out."

Xavier snarled at the mention of Aura. "There is no way someone can defy fate." Though doubt started to form in his mind as he thought about the events leading up to this day. Not everything matched up and with his son going against all orders and wishes Xavier gave him, the Demon King had no choice but to believe the crone. He shook his head at the thoughts and started out of the room, he would let the servants clean up the bloodstains on the floor.

Cora flexed her hands as she felt the magic return to her. An ache in her heart told her that Theresa no longer walked the earth. Cora knew that she could not let the sacrifice go to waste, so with a deep breath she demanded no tears from herself. She looked at Darius, "You need to put Alaster in chains." She looked up at the other Demon Hunter. "It's the only way his father will believe our story."

"I don't know if I trust him to do that." Alaster stepped back. "If I'm chained up and helpless then I can't help you fight."

Darius shrugged. "I won't bind your magic, but she's right, if you aren't restrained the king won't believe us."

"Fine, I swear if you use this against me, I will kill you. You should be happy I'm even working with you." Alaster crossed his arms. "I should be taking her home where she will be safe."

"Safe? Her father would just turn her back out." Darius shook his head. "She won't be safe until the king is dead." He summoned some chains and started to chain Alaster up. "We'll go to my quarters, because that's where he'll be expecting us. Especially since you are supposed to still be hurt." He held his hand out to her.

She took it, still wrapping the blanket around her instead of changing into the clothes. "Then let's go. Theresa is already gone from this world. That means he'll be looking for you soon."

In a shifting of magic they appeared in his room. Alaster looked around and made a disgusted noise. "Like to live on the high side do you?"

Cora made her way to the bed, her body feeling better, but still protesting in some spots, and wrapped herself in the silk sheets, lying on the bed. "Leave him alone, he wasn't forced to live in a cave or a poor village."

"Being Prince has its perks." Darius shrugged. "Cora, rest up while you can."

Cora closed her eyes as Alaster looked over at her. "Shouldn't she get dressed?"

"I'll flash clothes on before the king gets here." She yawned. "Sleep first."

Alaster nodded and moved to a corner to wait for the king, his eyes all for Cora.

"She really is a pretty one, isn't she?" Darius asked, making sure to pull a fur blanket over her, and watching as her body rose and fell as she slept.

Alaster nodded, "But there is so much more to her."

"Her strength, her will power, her fight." Darius laughed. "I could go on, but you know all her attributes. Does she know?"

Alaster shook his head, "No, I've managed to keep a lot of that secret from her. She just recently found out about her father wanting us married."

The thought of Alaster touching Cora made Darius' skin crawl. "I'm sure she loved that." He laughed trying to make light of it, but froze when the door opened and Xavier waltzed in.

"Darius, I heard you caught the trespasser." His

eyes flickered to the lump in the bed. "And got your whore back."

Darius shrugged and motioned to the corner where Alaster stood. "He was trying to rescue her from her hell. I thought it only appropriate that I take back what is mine."

Cora stirred under the blankets, but made no noise, just a restless sleep for the exhausted magic user. Everyone's eyes flickered to her. Xavier walked towards the bed. "She should go back to her hell."

"No." Darius stepped up behind his father.

Xavier glanced over his back. "You want to protect her? I already killed her sister, and she has proven useless to me."

Darius turned to see the fire flare a bit, glad the king did not notice and praying Cora held her temper long enough. "She is still useful to me." He shrugged. "Even without her magic I do enjoy her body." He glanced at the form in the bed. Feeling another flare of magic from her, he tensed.

Xavier's eyes went to the fire and he pushed past his son to see the violin still lying on the hearth of the fireplace. "You let her play still?"

"That's been here since you dragged her out of my room a week ago." He watched as his father picked up the instrument and started playing it. Xavier closed his eyes at the sweet sound as he drew the bow across the string. "Aura used to play by the fire for me, before she betrayed me and slept with the Demon Hunter."

"Aura is dead, because you killed her." Darius watched closely, moving to get behind his father, his hand on the hilt of his sword.

The king laughed as he played the haunting tune. "Because she betrayed me."

Darius pulled his sword out and swung at his father.

Xavier reacted within an instant, dropping the violin and drawing his own sword, blocking the attack.

146

"You dare betray me, your king?"

"You have been in reign long enough." Darius pushed against his father, pushing him back.

Xavier laughed and started to shift to his demon form. "You are not strong enough to defeat me."

"But I am." Cora whispered, rising from the bed, her eyes green flames as her magic swirled around her. The flames in the fireplace joined the swirls around her, as she moved closer to the demon, "Do not underestimate me like you did my mother."

He snarled at her, his wings flaring out, nearly filling the span of the room. "Your mother was weak."

Cora raised her hand and sent a ribbon of fire towards the demon, using it as a whip, cracking it at Xavier.

Xavier blocked with his wing, snarling as it burnt the leathery flesh. He glared over the top, his red eyes flashing dangerously at her. Darius took his chance. Using Cora as a distraction, he slammed his blade into Xavier's shoulder. The demon snarled as Darius twisted the blade, giving Cora her chance to throw more fire at Xavier.

Xavier cried as the fire bit into him and the steel in him burned. Cora tried to think as he came rampaging towards her. Calling harder on her magic, she started to pull on the heat in Xavier's body, watching as Darius shoved Xavier to the ground, pinning him there with the sword. Cora moved towards the demon, avoiding the flapping wings and the struggle, concentrating on the heat she felt flowing through him. The body began to burn from the inside out. Black cracks formed in the skin and angry orange and red rivulets tore it apart. The smell of burning flesh filled the room as the body started to crumble and turn to coals.

Cora pulled her magic back into her, before retrieving the sword. She knelt down on one knee.

Bowing her head, she offered the sword to Darius. "Long live the king." The fires around her extinguished as Darius approached her. He took the sword from her, and sheathed it. He pulled her up by her arm and swept in to give her a deep kiss. She melted into him, placing a hand on his chest to balance herself.

"Long live the queen." He whispered when he pulled back. She grabbed his shirt pulling him in for another kiss.

Alaster cleared his throat and Darius pulled back, wrapping a possessive arm around Cora's waist. "You want to untie me so I don't have to watch this? I do believe you two still have some work cut out for you. The Demon hunters are still planning on attacking, you might want to go make a treaty with Lucas, remove some bonds, and you know, act as a queen and king?"

Cora tried not to roll her eyes and went to unchain him. "Thank you, for everything." She kissed his cheek, pulling back with a smile.

Alaster stepped up to Cora and kissed her cheek, lingering for a moment long than she would have liked. "Shall we go see your father? I'm sure he would like to know that you are alive."

"Right, I'm sure." She snorted. "More likely he'll be glad that the war is over and I'm in a place of power."

Cora took a deep breath and walked into the main room to meet with Lucas. She had dressed in traditional demon hunting clothing; the tight leather clung to her legs, her weapons apparent, her arms covered in leather guards over her long sleeve shirt. Darius stood by her side, free of his weapons while Alaster stood behind them.

Lucas walked in a few seconds after and looked over the trio. "This is not what I expected." He stared at Cora. "You are dressed as one of us, and yet you stand with one of them."

"Xavier is dead and I stand at Darius' side as

queen. To rule." She crossed her arms, and watched as her father paced in front of the fire. "It is time for change, Father. Our kind will be free, no longer bound by demon magic."

He laughed. "You say that now, but what is to keep you from being corrupted by his magic?" He pointed at Darius, who stood there without blinking.

"Simple, ask him who killed Xavier."

Lucas turned towards Darius, waiting.

"Cora did, through her magic of fire." He shrugged. "She would easily be able to outclass my magic and kill me if I was to turn on her."

Alaster nodded. "She has shown great strength through her magic, and if anyone can rule by a demon's side it is your daughter."

"You willingly give your betrothed away?" Lucas snapped. "You who will not be accepted by either kind?"

Cora laughed. "The time of who will and will not be accepted is over. Alaster has used his talent to help free me."

"And what of Theresa? Where is her body Cora?"

Grief tore through her at the casual mention of her sister's body. "The crone has it, and is preparing it for a proper burial. Theresa gave her life so that I could get away and kill the king." She whispered. "There is no greater sacrifice. Now, if you would, we have drawn up a treaty between our people that I think will please you." She held her hand out to Darius who handed her the scroll and she placed on the table between her father and herself.

CHAPTER TWELVE

Cora stood in front of the mirror, her fingers dancing along her flat, naked stomach, the flames of the fire casting shadows against her skin. Tonight would be the night, she would dance again with her violin, filling the square with music, and then be bound by magic to Darius. With a smile she donned a shirt and pulled on her corset, one Darius had ordered for her. Red threads represented the magic she held within her, the black made her pale skin striking and her hair seem brighter. She pulled the skirts over her legs and bustled them up to keep them out from under her feet. Finally she pulled the mask off the mirror and placed it over her face, tying it under her hair. She missed this part of her, the Gypsy Lady, and refused to let Darius tell her to stay home. She held her hand out and the violin appeared, and then used her magic to take her to the stage in a puff of smoke.

The sun kissed the horizon, just going down as she appeared and played her first note. The sweet sound echoed against the forest and mountains of the surrounding area, and she smiled as people turned to her, gasping of her return. Questions filled the air as she started to play and dance. She never answered people's questions, not willing to give away her secrets.

Alaster stood at the back of the crowd watching Cora dance. Part of him yearned to be the one to take her home tonight. Rumors told him of the wedding planned at the castle tonight and then Darius and Cora would be as one.

"Jealous?" Darius asked appearing beside him, his eyes all for his future wife.

Alaster shrugged. "I'm still an outcast in my own right."

"Maybe you'll find your love." Darius smiled. "There is a time and a place for everything."

"You say that because you are marrying one of the creatures of fate now, you can change it as you will."

"Oh no, I can't, but she can. She knows the consequences though, and I highly doubt she'll risk it. How are the Demon Hunters dealing with the loss of Theresa?"

"They buried her and haven't spoken about her since. They keep to themselves about it. I think Lucas is consumed with guilt over everything that he has done to those girls." Alaster shook his head. "Shame he didn't know what either of them were capable of."

The crowd burst into applause when Cora finished her dance. "Yeah, damn shame." Darius made his way through the crowd. Some people greeted him, some shied away, and some sneered. He held his hand up to the stage. "I am glad that the Gypsy Lady has chosen to bless us with her presence once again. It has been a great honor to watch you dance and spread your hope to the people once more."

Alaster walked way from the crowd, refusing to listen to Darius go on about times of peace and a new hope with the queen. He knew it would take years for the land and the people to heal. He had no such hope of things turning out otherwise.

About the Author

A.L. Kessler is an up and coming author, with her first short story, *Keeper*, published in the anthology *Evernight Vol. II*. Since she was a teenager she's loved weaving stories and spinning tales. When she's not at the beck-and-call of the Lord and Lady of the House, two black cats by the names of Jynx and Sophie, playing with her daughter, or killing creepers and mining all the things with her husband of Four years, she's either reading, participating in NaNoWriMo, or writing in her Blog Writing Rambles.

Connect with me online:

Website: www.amylkessler.com
Facebook: alkesslerauthor
Twitter: @A_L_Kessler
Goodreads: A.L. Kessler

Also Available

Keeper (Available in Evernight Volume 2)

Coming Soon:

In The Light of The Moon: Book One in the Dark Wars Series-
Stripped of all control, shifter Kassity has no choice but to be a killer for Lucius. Obeying the vampire from the shadows was simply her way of life, until Jax comes to town and brings trouble with him. When her panther half recognizes Jax as her fated mate, Kassity must deal with betrayal, secrets and Lucius in order to be with him.

CPSIA information can be obtained at www.ICGtesting.com
Printed in the USA
LVOW05s1640090414

381020LV00019B/1223/P

9 781482 333121